MANVERS ROAD STAR

JON FRANKLIN

Follow me at:
Instagram: jonfranklinauthor
BlueSky: Jon Franklin @racingtales.bsky.social
X: Jon Franklin@JonFranklin63

Biography portrait: Linnea Franklin
Interior design: Damian Jackson
Cover design: Xee_designs1

First print edition 2025.

To my daughter, Linnea

ABOUT THIS BOOK

Manvers Road Star is the sequel to *Shouting the Odds,* published in August, 2021. While it is as a stand-alone novel, if you have previously read *Shouting the Odds*, you will have a better understanding of *Manvers Road Star* as a consequence. For reference, a cast of characters page is included at the back of the book.

— JON FRANKLIN, APRIL 2025.

EPIGRAPHS

'A horse is the projection of peoples' dreams about themselves – strong, powerful, beautiful and it gives us the capability of giving us escape from our mundane existence.'

— PAM BROWN, HORSE PSYCHOLOGY; UNDERSTANDING EQUINE BEHAVIOUR (1992).

'Horses change lives. They give our young people confidence and self-esteem. They provide peace and tranquillity to troubled souls. They give us hope.'

— TONI ROBINSON, SPEECH AT EQUINE ASSISTED THERAPY CONFERENCE (2007).

'Horse racing is a mirror of life. It's beautiful. It's brutal. It's pure. It's real.'

— BOB NEUMEIER, NORTH AMERICAN HORSE RACING BROADCASTER AND COMMENTATOR.

‘A horse gallops with his lungs, perseveres with his heart and wins with his character.’

— FEDERICO TESIO, FARMER,
RACEHORSE BREEDER, OWNER AND
TRAINER.

‘People wouldn’t understand why my mamma would have this blind kid out doing things like cutting wood for the fire. But her thinking was: he may be blind, but he isn’t stupid.’

— RAY CHARLES, LEGENDARY SOUL,
JAZZ AND BLUES ARTIST.

‘Everyone has special needs, like Father, who has to carry a little packet of artificial sweetener tablets around with him to put in his coffee to stop him from getting fat, or Mrs Peters who wears a beige coloured hearing-aid, or Siobhan, who has glasses so thick they give you a headache if you borrow them, and none of these people are Special Needs, even if they have special needs.’

— CHRISTOPHER BOONE, IN MARK
HADDON’S, THE CURIOUS INCIDENT OF
THE DOG IN THE NIGHT-TIME.

PART I

1

★ ANDY COOPER ★

OCTOBER, 1996

Before he passed away, dad put on a bet on my behalf for twenty-five pounds. All seven horses won and the returns came to three-hundred and twenty-seven thousand pounds. Unofficially, this makes me the wealthiest postman in the East Midlands. I'm sitting in the living room of the flat I rent above Sanjay's off-licence, when the telephone rings. My girlfriend, Rita, calls out from the adjoining room.

'I'll get it.' A moment later she pokes her head round the door. 'It's Laura. Her and Duke want to know if we'd like to go to Colwick Park races on Saturday?'

* * *

Three days later, the four of us exit a cab outside the racecourse entrance. Though I enjoy a bet at my local bookies on Manvers Road, I've never been to a racecourse before, let alone to my local one. I take in my surroundings and as we enter through the turnstiles, the sun pokes its head out from behind the clouds, illuminating the pathway that leads up to the grandstand.

Racegoers of all ages pass us by, many dressed in their Sunday best. Others sit chatting with one another on wooden benches, scattered every few yards along the pathway. A bit further on, I hear the sound of clinking glasses and laughter ringing out from a marquee bar called Jonny's. Around halfway to the grandstand we come upon a six-piece jazz band, huddled together on a small stage. The bandleader is wearing a trilby hat and a snazzy shirt covered with racehorses.

'Good afternoon, we're the Basford Players,' he announces. 'Welcome to Colwick Park!' He takes a sip from his pint and counts in the band. I recognise the opening bars of 'The Sunny Side of the Street.' The music puts a spring in my step and continuing along the pathway, the smell of fried onions and charcoal-grilled burgers wafts across the race-course lawn.

As we reach the grandstand, the sun disappears behind some clouds. To the left of the entrance, an elderly Timeform vendor is doing a lively trade, shoe-horned as he is between a Mr Whippy ice cream van and a Tote betting booth. A couple of minutes later we reach the parade ring, where our arrival is greeted by the clip-clop sound of horses' hooves on tarmac. Rita turns to me and smiles. 'So, what do you think?'

I meet her gaze. Her hair is braided with colourful beads and gathered in a bun and the auburn-coloured coat she's wearing compliments her latte complexion.

'Well, it beats Meadow Lane on a cold November evening,' I say, all dead-pan. She bursts into laughter and playfully slaps my shoulder.

'Seriously, Andy! I'm curious?'

'Seriously?' I say. 'I think it's brilliant.'

The truth is, it was love at first sight. I feel like I've climbed through the big screen up on the wall at Manvers Road bookies and arrived in a technicolour racing wonderland.

* * *

That afternoon, I place my first bets since my recent windfall. I back two winners, though I end up slightly down on the day. After the last race I find myself separated from the others, carried along by the tide of the crowd to the edge of the winners enclosure. A jovial racecourse official congratulates the winning connections and ushers them on to the podium. The winning jockey and trainer join them and handshakes and hugs are exchanged. The glee on their faces speaks to me and while I find myself happy for them, I feel strangely envious too. The racecourse photographer steps forward to compose his picture. He turns on his flash-unit and *boom* - an idea strikes me, as though triggered by the blast of tungsten light. A pair of hands covers my eyes from behind me.

'So, this is where you got to?' says Rita. 'All good?'

She removes her hands. I turn to face her and smile. 'All good. In fact, never been better.'

* * *

One week later, I'm sitting in the driver's seat of a white Ford transit van outside Manvers Road bookies. I hired it from a car dealership place just round the corner. I do a quick headcount in the rear-view mirror: Glen, Big Les, Duke, Des, One-Armed Bruce. Rita is sat in the front beside me. We're just waiting on Lee and Sammy Chan. Just at that moment I see them, locking up the Flying Dragon Takeaway restaurant, of which they are the owners.

Des slides open the side door as they reach the van. ‘Morning fellas’, he says.

‘Morning Des’, says Sammy, helping his dad into the van. 'Has he said where he’s taking us yet?’

Des casually shrugs his shoulders and smiles. ‘Search me.’

* * *

Only Rita and Duke are in on my surprise. All I told the others at the King Billy the other night was to meet me here at ten o’clock in the morning.

‘So, where are we going, Andy?’ says Glen, from two rows back. ‘I’m not sure I like mystery road trips.’

‘If he told us where we were going, it wouldn’t be a mystery road trip would it, you berk’, quips Big Les. Duke and One-Armed laugh from the row of seats behind me.

I turn the key in the ignition and the engine starts up. ‘You’ll find out soon enough, Glen.’

* * *

We leave Nottingham in the direction of Arnold on the A614. A few minutes later, Big Les pipes up. ‘I know where we’re heading!’

I make eye contact with him in the rear-view mirror. ‘Go on then.’

‘Southwell races?’

‘Sorry Les – another time maybe.’

‘You’re enjoying this, aren’t you?’ says Rita.

I say nothing, but return her smile with a glint in my eye.

I forge on passed the turn-offs for Calverton, Bildsworth, Farnsfield and Bildsthorpe, before taking the exit for Lidgett in the direction of Edwinstowe at Rufford Abbey. Before long I slow to a crawl along a private road. Five minutes later, I drive the van up a short, steep driveway. The sign displaying the name of the property is obscured by an overgrown hedgerow. I pull in to the gravel stoned courtyard and park between a red tractor and a mud-splattered Land Rover. Directly in front of us stands an old stone cottage. To our left and right are two giant barns, one of which is stacked from top to bottom with hay bales.

'Okay', I say from the driver's compartment. 'Everybody out'. Everyone exits the van.

The air is thin and rich with horse manure. Big Les scratches his head. 'So, what are we doing on a farm in the middle of the Sherwood Forest?'

Removing a rucksack from the front seat, Rita and I look at him and smile. 'That's what you're about to find out. C'mon.'

I lead them past the stone cottage to the edge of a field. We pass a long white table in the shade of a giant oak tree, with chairs scattered around it. The field is hemmed in by a stretch of white railings. The outer width of turf on the inside of the rail has been ploughed and laid with an all-weather gallop. I turn and face my friends.

'Okay, a starter for ten. Which Nottinghamshire trainer has won the Cambridgeshire Handicap no less than four times?'

Glen pips Big Les to the answer by a short-head. 'Ray Baldwin?'

'Correct Glen. And for a bonus point, do know where his stables are?'

Duke sends Rita a coy smile. She winks back at him.

'Near Edwinstowe,' says Glen. 'In fact, not a million miles from ...'

Big Les stares at me. 'Blimey, is this his gaff?'

'Yes, it is,' I say. 'C'mon.' I wander down to the gallops. Everyone follows suit. Leaning my hands on the rail, I turn around and addressing everyone, say, 'Now. Listen and watch.'

* * *

Out of view to our left comes the sound of hooves, quickly gathering speed. It becomes louder and louder and then *whooooossshh!* A chestnut racehorse thunders past, scattering a wave of fibresand in our direction. The hair on the back of my neck stands on end. Des gasps. Everyone looks on in silence as the horse is cantered back towards us. The horse's rider removes their goggles. They reveal the smiling face of a girl in her early twenties. She has green eyes and strands of jet-black hair peak out from around the edges of her riding helmet. She greets me in a soft Irish brogue. 'Hello, Andy.'

'Hi Ellie.' I turn and face my friends. 'So, what do you think of her?'

Sammy Chan is the first to react. Gazing at Ellie, he says, 'She's a looker all right.'

I turn to Ellie and sigh. 'I apologise for my friend.' Ellie rolls her eyes. I look at Sammy. 'I don't mean her, you plonker - I mean the *horse*.'

Big Les looks the beautiful chestnut horse up and down. 'She's a "she", is she?'

Stooping on all fours, Glen seeks confirmation. 'Yes,' he says. 'She's a she all right.'

'And a real beauty at that', adds Des.

'So', I say, pausing for effect for a moment. 'What would you say if I told you that this beautiful filly is now ours?'

* * *

As Ellie walks our horse back towards the stables, five stunned faces gawp back at me. For once in his life, Sammy Chan is speechless.

One Armed Bruce appears sceptical. 'Is this some kind of a wind up? Okay, where are the hidden cameras?'

I can't help laughing. 'No, it's not a wind up. Let me explain. Last week I went to Colwick Park races. I'd never been before. It was brilliant. And while I was there, an idea struck me - to buy us a racehorse.'

'Bloody hell!' says Glen.

Des rushes towards me and embraces me like a long-lost son. 'I've dreamt of owning a racehorse for as long as I can remember!' he says.

'You're welcome, Des,' I say, a little overcome. 'Losing my parents last year was tough. Rita and Duke know what it almost did to me. Looking back, I don't think I could have got through it all without the support I got from you lot.'

Duke steps forward and gives me a bear hug. Lee Chan approaches. Placing his hands together like an eastern mystic, he slowly bows. 'Thank you, Andy. Big shock. Nice shock! Now I think I need to sit down.'

'You're welcome, Lee,' I say, smiling.

'Thanks Andy', says his son, Sammy. 'It's unbelievable! Sammy turns to Lee. 'Er, are you alright Dad?'

'I'm fine', he says. 'Big shock. Nice shock. All good!'

I rest my hand on Lee's shoulder – and point towards the large table under the oak tree. 'Let's all go and sit down over there. C'mon.'

* * *

Once everyone is seated, I open my rucksack and take out two bottles of champagne. Rita circles the table and hands out plastic champagne flutes. I pop open one of the bottles and turn to Duke. 'Perhaps you could tell everyone how Laura helped me turn my idea into reality?'

'Sure,' says Duke. 'So, when Andy told me he was interested in buying a racehorse, I suggested he had a chat with Laura. You see, her uncle is Ray Baldwin - and as chance would have it, he'd just bought some horses for syndication.'

I take over. 'Laura drove me up here last week and introduced me to Ray. By then, I had a pretty good idea about what kind of racehorse I was looking for.'

Big Les takes a swig of bubbly. 'And what kind is that?'

'I told Ray I was interested in a horse that would be suited by the straight six-furlong course at Colwick Park – you know, so we can all go and watch her run.'

'Nice one', says Sammy.

'Ray recommended the filly we just saw. She's a half-sister to two winners, both over six furlongs. Her pedigree suggests she'll run best on good ground. Ray's trained many of her family. According to him, they've all been genuine and straightforward, so that was that. I bought her.' I pause to light a cigarette. 'Now, here's the best part.' I take a swig of bubbly. 'I've asked Ray to lay her out for us to have a "touch" at Colwick Park next spring'.

Big Les empties his glass. 'What, like our very own coup?'

'Yeah,' I say, smiling.

'How cool is that?', says Glen.

Sammy laughs. 'Andy Cooper – Nottingham's answer to Barney Curley!'

Everyone joins in, myself included. I see the glee in everyone's eyes and feel a warm glow inside. 'I think it's time I introduced you all to Ray. He'll be over at the stables with Ellie. Bring your glasses if you've not finished your bubbly. There's something I need your help with before we drive home.'

* * *

A couple of minutes later we arrive at the stabling area. It's U-shaped, immaculately tidy and has horse boxes on three sides. There are thirty boxes and all but a couple are occupied. I see Ray and Ellie. They're discussing a large bay horse stood in front of his box. When Ray sees us, he says something to Ellie and she leads the horse away. Ray waves us over. As we approach, Big Les and Glen appear hesitant. 'What's wrong?' I say.

Big Les looks down at his shoes. 'We're just a bit in awe of him, that's all.'

Glen nods in agreement. 'Ray is something of a local hero, you know.'

I place my arms around both of their shoulders and smile. 'More the reason for not keeping him waiting then, eh?'

* * *

The first thing one notices about Ray Baldwin is the awkward way in which he carries himself, according to Laura, the result of a riding accident some years back. His injury doesn't appear to have left him in any pain however and his demeanour is open and friendly. Ray is of average height and build and wears a flat cap, framing an untidy thatch of wispy, silver-tinged hair. He's wearing a waxed jacket, a pair of brown corduroys and wellington boots. Ellie stands at his side. We stop in a semi-circle before them. Ray's eyes are a piercing blue, mischievous and playful, and when he speaks its in a gravelly, north Nottinghamshire accent.

'Welcome to Nine Oaks Stables, everyone.'

'Thanks, Mr Baldwin', reply Glen and Big Les in unison.

'Please, call me Ray,' he says. 'I believe you've all met Ellie?' Everyone nods. 'Ellie McGovern here is my Head Lass, my righthand woman so to speak. So long as your filly is trained here, she will be in Ellie's care.' He looks at each of us in turn and smiles. 'I see you're all enjoying a glass of the "good stuff"?'

Rita takes the hint and offers Ray and Ellie a plastic champagne flute each.

'There you go', I say, pouring the remainder of the second bottle into their glasses. 'Ray, is it be possible to see our filly again before we head back to town? You see, I need everyone's help with something.'

'Of course,' he says. 'Ellie, walk her out here, would you?'

Ellie fetches our filly from her box and leads her over. My heart melts, just like it did the first time I set eyes on her last week. She has a striking white blaze that runs the length of her face, but the thing that strikes me most about her is her beautiful, tranquil eyes. I fumble in my coat pocket and bring out a bag of carrots. 'May I?'

Ray smiles. 'Be my guest.'

I approach her cautiously. She tilts her head slightly, watching my every move. 'Here you are,' I say, holding out a carrot under her mouth.

She takes the bait. As she munches the carrot, I ruffle her mane - and when she's eaten up, I hold out my fingers under her nose and she licks them. I tilt my head slowly towards her and she does the same.

'Can I give her one, Andy?' asks Des.

I look at Ray. He nods. 'She won't get fat on those', he says, laughing.

I hand Des the bag of carrots.

One-Armed turns to me and says, 'Have you named her yet?'

'No,' I say. 'That's what I want everyone's help with. Any suggestions?' Names spring forth. One or two are just plain daft, while others would definitely struggle to get past the Jockey Club names committee.

'What about Manvers Road Star?' suggests Big Les.

'That's it!' I say – 'it's perfect, Les!' Duke pats Big Les on the back. It's the first time any of us have seen Big Les blush.

'If I may Andy, I'd like to propose a toast?' says Duke.

'Be my guest,' I say.

Duke raises his plastic champagne flute and everyone follows suit. 'To Manvers Road Star: The Queen of Sneinton!'

Everyone laughs and applauds, before repeating Duke's words as one.

'Manvers Road Star: The Queen of Sneinton!'

2

★ ANDY ★

In time, the name Manvers Road Star morphs into the nickname 'Star'. Using her initials MRS was short lived, after causing too much confusion - like the time we were all sat together around a table at the King Billy one night. Before heading to the bar to buy a round, I told everyone that '*Mrs has eaten up well following a morning of light training.*' When I returned with our drinks, Big Les wasn't the only one who was under the impression that Rita had enjoyed a wholesome lunch earlier, following a morning at the gym.

'Project Star' is a real team effort: I came up with the money, Laura came up with the trainer and Ray came up with the horse. Big Les came up with the name and after everyone else drew a blank, the Chans came up with the design of our distinctive racing silks. These are presented to the rest of us at a special unveiling at the Flying Dragon one night after closing time. Upon our arrival, the Chans position themselves behind the restaurant counter. Sammy invites the rest of us to sit on a long bench opposite on the customer side, as though waiting on a large takeaway order. Once everyone is seated,

Lee unveils four beige napkins that he's stapled together, onto which Sammy had drawn his design with colour marker pens. Using a chopstick as a makeshift presentation tool, he talks us through their creation.

'We propose green as the main colour of the silks, overlaid with nine red stars, each one representing a syndicate member.'

'Nice one', says Des.

'Yeah,' says Big Les. 'Like the Agha Khan's silks, only better!'

Sammy smiles. 'Cheers, Les.'

'What's the thinking behind the choice of colours?' says Duke.

Sammy explains. 'Red and green are considered very lucky colours - not only by dad and I, but by the entire Chinese race.'

One-Armed chips in. 'And one point four billion people can't be wrong!'

Lee Chan smiles. Everyone laughs. Sammy continues. 'Red symbolises happiness, success and good fortune. Green symbolises money and wealth. Kind of appropriate, we thought.' Sammy turns and looks at me. 'So, what do you think?'

'Honestly?' I say.

'Yeah – honestly.'

'Well, what's good for the Chinese, is good enough for me! I think they're great, Sammy!'

'Cheers', he says.

'Seriously mate, I'm impressed. Turning to his dad, I add, 'nice job, Mr Chan.'

Lee Chan bows.

'They're fantastic,' adds Big Les.

The Chans beam with pride. 'Thanks everyone', says

Sammy, adding, 'presentation concluded.' He folds up the napkin and carefully places it behind the counter.

Then Lee Chan turns to us all and says, 'So – who's hungry?'

* * *

The team ethos behind 'Project Star' is completed by Duke's contribution. Being a solicitor, he offers to take care of all legal matters, such as registering Star's name with the Jockey Club, and ensuring that our syndicate name is added to the official register of racehorse owners. He also helps me draft a simple document covering the terms of co-ownership, copies of which I hand out to everyone at the King Billy one night. Also present is Ray, who I invite along to talk about his campaign for Star in the run-up to our 'Colwick Park coup' next spring.

Holding a copy of the document in one hand and my pint in the other, I address the group. 'This document makes us equal owners in Star. It also entitles each of you to a 12.5% share of any prize money she may earn during the year ahead. When the year is up, we'll meet again and review the situation, based upon her performances on the track.'

'Perhaps she'll attract interest from one of the sheikhs?' says Big Les, his eyes lighting up with dollar signs.

'You never know', I say, smiling. 'Either way, your co-ownership of Star is entirely risk free – I'll meet all the training and other costs during the year ahead. All the details are in here,' I point at the document. 'Any questions?'

Sammy pipes up. 'Yeah, I have one. When will Star make her debut?'

Lee Chan says, 'and how much can we have on?'

A murmur of excitement spreads around the table. 'I think

this might be a good time for me to hand over to Ray,' I say. Ray takes a swig of beer and raises himself to his feet.

'So,' he says, 'as you already know, my job is to get your girl nicely handicapped for a race at Colwick Park next May. Before that, Star will need to run three times. The chief handicapper will then assess her ability based upon what he has seen and allocate her a handicap rating, befitting of these three performances.'

'What do you mean by "nicely handicapped"?' says Sammy.

Ray turns and faces me. 'Can I be blunt with everyone, Andy?'

I take a swig from my pint and smile. 'Be as blunt as you like, Ray.'

'Okay – so during Star's first three runs, my job is to conceal her true ability from the handicapper – indulge in a little *smoke screens and mirrors*, so to speak. I'll explain more about how I intend to do that later. If I do my job properly, it means that when she enters the starting stalls at Colwick Park next May, Star will be several pounds "well in". That is to say, running off a lower handicap rating than her true ability warrants, providing you all with the best possible chance of landing some big bets at decent odds.'

Big Les rubs his hands together with glee and turns to Des. 'I like what I'm hearing.'

Des smiles broadly. 'Me too.'

'How do you conceal her true ability from the handicapper without breaking the rules of racing?' says One-Armed.

Ray takes a swig from his pint. 'That's a good question, one I can best answer with a question of my own. What race conditions has Andy said should suit Star best?'

'A straight six furlongs on good ground,' says Des.

'Correct. So, on her debut, we run her somewhere that won't suit her at all – like the left-turning oval course down the road at Southwell on the all-weather. You see, the handicapper can only assess a horse based upon what he sees - and what he'll most likely see watching her run at Southwell is a horse struggling with the conditions, especially as I'll only have her seventy percent fit on the day. All we should hope for on her debut is that she loads into the stalls without any fuss.' A murmur of approval travels around the table.

'Brilliant,' whispers Big Les in Sammy's ear. 'This fella knows his onions.' Sammy smiles and nods.

Ray continues. 'For her second and third races, we'll run her in other conditions that will prevent her from showing her best form - rain-softened ground, racing right-handed, that kind of thing – so that when the handicapper comes to allocate Star an opening handicap rating, he cannot fail to give her a lowly one.' He pauses for a second and takes a swig from his pint. 'Then, in preparation for her big day at Colwick Park, I'll put her into training on my six- furlong grass gallops. Slowly but surely, Ellie and I will build up her fitness, bringing her to peak condition on the day of the race. *This* is what I mean by getting Star nicely handicapped. And in answer to your other question, I'd say save all of your "hard-earnt" until May!'

I glance around the table. Everyone is mesmerised. Glen turns to face me. 'May I say a few words, Andy?'

'Sure, Glen.'

'I'd just like to thank you Ray on behalf of all of us for coming here and sharing your wisdom with us,' he says. 'I think it's fair to say that we have an exciting few months ahead!' A murmur of agreement sweeps around the table. Ray smiles. 'You're very kind, Glen. Thank you.'

'So, everyone,' says Glen, 'please join me in raising a

glass to Ray, who, in the spirit of another Sherwood Forest legend, is going to help this band of merry men rob those rich bookies!' Everyone erupts with laughter.

'That's a flattering comparison,' says Ray. 'And one I'll do my utmost to live up to!'

Looking around the table, I experience a feeling of complete contentment. I feel proud too, proud to have set something in motion that my friends and I will never forget - a lifelong memory for us to share forever. All of have witnessed the occasional coup play out down at Manvers Road bookies - but the thing that will make this coup seem very different is that we won't be on the outside looking in. We will be its instigators.

I feel a tap on the shoulder. It's Duke. 'Roll on May, eh?' he says.

'Yeah. All roads lead to Colwick Park!'

Duke smiles - and lighting one of his cigarillos, looks at my near empty glass. 'Fancy a refill?'

'Yeah, go on then.'

Operation Star is underway. What could possibly go wrong?

3

★ ANDY ★

It's a bitter, cold January morning, and for the first time in my life, I'm Sanjay's first customer of the day. Clutching a copy of the Racing Post, I scurry back up the stairway to the flat, throw off my coat and spread the paper out on the living room table. I flick through it impatiently, in search of today's card at Southwell. I find it and scrolling down the page to the 2.45 race, look through the declared entries and there she is – number 5, Manvers Road Star.

'Rita. Look!' Rita appears from the bathroom wrapped in a towel. I point at the miniature colour graphic besides Star's name, displaying our red and green racing silks. I pinch myself to make sure that I'm not dreaming.

'Bloody hell!' she says, 'it's so exciting!'

* * *

We arrive at Southwell Racecourse early afternoon. After parking the transit van, I ask Rita, Big Les, Glen, Des, Duke, One-Armed, Sammy and Lee Chan to line up outside the

Owners and Trainers entrance. Starting with Rita, I pin a shiny green *owner* badge to each of their coat lapels, making my way along the line like a sergeant major dishing out medals to his troops. Once I'm done, I look at each of them in turn and smile. 'Everybody ready?' Eight faces nod back at me. 'Okay,' I say. 'Then let's go.'

* * *

Knowing in advance that Manvers Road Star won't be making a winning debut does nothing to dampen our first taste of the owner's experience. It may be just another dreary, mid-week meeting at Southwell to many, but to us it feels like Derby Day at Epsom. Twenty minutes before Star's race, in the manner of Michael Tabor, John Magnier and the other Coolmore cohorts, we stride purposefully into the parade ring. Ray sees me and waves us over. As we approach, he looks each of us up and down in turn.

'Blimey!' he says. 'If there was a prize for the "best turned out" connections, my money would be on you lot!' Everyone laughs. 'Look', he adds, pointing towards the entrance from the pre-parade ring. 'Here she comes'. In walks Star, flanked by Ellie. Ellie holds her close, whispering sweet nothings into her ear.

As soon as Star and Ellie have passed, a colourful posse of jockeys' fan out of the weighing room into the parade ring. One of them is instantly recognisable due to his red and green silks. He strides over and joins us. Ray places his arm around his shoulder and smiles.

'This here everyone is Callum Teak.' The cherubic jockey nods and simultaneously slaps his whip down his riding boots. 'Callum is an apprentice I use regularly. Star will be safe in his hands.'

'Pleased to meet you all,' says Callum. His words are met with a chorus of greetings.

'How do you like the silks?' says Lee Chan.

'Very smart', says Callum.

'Smart, yes – and lucky too', says Lee. 'The colour red symbolises success and the colour green symbolises money and wealth.'

'Oh, right', says Callum. 'Nice one.'

'Success, money and wealth', Lee repeats - before lowering his voice to a whisper. Cupping his hand over Callum's left ear, he says, 'not today, though.' Lee catches Callum's eye and winks. For a split second, I'm worried Lee is going to slip a wad of notes into Callum's palm, but fortunately he doesn't and I'm spared further embarrassment by the sound of the bell.

'Jockeys please mount', comes the announcement over the parade ring tannoy.

Ray joins us. 'Callum?'

'Yes, Mr Baldwin?'

'A quick word in your shell-like, please,' he says.

* * *

Lee needn't have worried about Star out-running her odds. Though she breaks well, her wide draw gives her little chance and as Ray had predicted, she is unable to handle the sharp left turning track. Running slightly wide in the home straight to avoid the worst of the kickback, she finishes eighth of eleven, beaten twelve lengths.

* * *

Two weeks later, Star runs again on the all-weather track at Lingfield Park in Surrey. We watch the race together on the big screen at Manvers Road bookies gathered around Des, sat in his usual place on a stool at the end of the betting counter. It's raining hard at the leafy Surrey track. Up on the big screen, all eyes are on Star as she's led forward by two stall handlers. She enters the stalls with the minimum fuss.

'She shows a good temperament', says Des. 'A definite plus for Colwick Park in May.'

I nod at Des and offer him a cigarette. He accepts. The gates spring open and Star breaks well, but as soon as she is off a straight line, she begins to struggle. Des says, 'look at her action. She doesn't like the surface, see?'

I look at him and smile. 'You could have worked for Timeform,' I say.

Des laughs. Two days previously, Des had been in to hospital for a check-up following a heart complaint. He'd had us all a bit worried, so it was good to see him in such good form. Star ends up being beaten about nine lengths.

Duke sidles over and lights one of his cigarillos. 'Never have I been happier seeing a horse finish eighth.' Des and I laugh. 'That run deserves a celebratory drink. C'mon everyone, my shout.'

With that, everyone files out of the bookies. It might have been raining in Surrey, but Sneinton is bathed in winter sunshine.

On the way to the King Billy, Duke falls into stride with me. 'Two runs, two duck eggs - I'd say things are going nicely to script, wouldn't you?'

'Yes, Duke', I say, smiling – 'they certainly are.'

4

★ ANDY ★

'Happy Birthday!' I'm stood in the entrance to the bedroom holding out a tray. Through bleary eyes, Rita raises her head off the pillow and squints in my direction. I take a few steps into the room. 'Breakfast in bed, birthday girl. Here we go.'

'Careful, Andy,' she says, seeing me struggling with the tray.

* * *

Since dad's death in October, Rita and I have been more or less living together. It isn't anything we've actually sat down and talked about, it just kind of happened. I place the tray on the bedside table and park myself on the side of the bed.

'Thank you, this is really nice. What time is it?'

'Don't worry about the time. It's Friday. We're both off, remember?'

Rita yawns and sends me a smile. 'Oh yeah. Come here,' she says.

I lean in towards her. She takes my face in her hands and

kisses me. I smile and pass her the breakfast tray. Leant against her coffee mug is an envelope. I can barely contain myself for excitement. Apparently, it shows.

'What is it?' says Rita.

'What?' I say.

'Andy?'

'Nothing,' I say, 'it's just, well, you know how bad I am at keeping surprises.'

'Struggling, are you?' she says, smiling.

'Yeah – just a bit.'

Rita takes a sip of orange juice. 'Wow, freshly squeezed. I'm impressed.'

'The envelope', I say. 'Open it'. She picks it up and does as I say. 'Sorry about the cheesy card.'

Rita smiles. It features an illustration of a giant teddy bear clutching a heart. As she opens the envelope, two tickets fall out onto the tray. She picks one up and reads it: 'Saturday, February 4th. East Midlands Airport – Rome Fiumicino?' Her jaw drops. 'That's today?'

'That's right', I say.

She holds her hand up to her mouth. 'Andy! That's the best surprise, *ever!'*

I smile. 'A taxi will be here at twelve.'

* * *

We're sat together on the terracotta tiled veranda of our Amalfi Coast hotel. The veranda is decorated with softly glowing fairy lights and juts out over an olive grove. Beyond that lies an expanse of Mediterranean Sea. For a while we just sit there sipping our champagne, watching it turn a velvety purple colour in the slowly fading light. It's after ten but still warm. Lifting the champagne bottle from its ice-box, I refill our glasses.

Rita looks at me. 'I could get used to this,' she says.

'Me too. Just as well you don't just love me for my money,' I say, winking.

'About that,' she says, coyly.

I raise my glass. 'Happy Birthday, Rita.'

'Thank you.'

'You're welcome.'

* * *

The following day we head in to Rome. Our driver drops us off on the edge of the Piazza Navona. 'Okay - The Coliseum, St Peter's Basilica or the Pantheon? The choice is yours,' I say.

'Er …'

'Or, perhaps we could spend the afternoon at Capannelle?'

'Capannelle?' she says.

'Yeah. Rome's racecourse. There happens to be a meeting today. First race is at –'

Rita cuts me short. 'Nothing involving racing today, Andy, okay?'

'I was only kidding – half kidding, perhaps …'

'All right. What about a visit to the Coliseum and then lunch somewhere?'

* * *

That night, lying in bed together, I turn to Rita. Facing her, I say, 'can I ask you something?'

She turns around. 'Of course – anything.'

'You are okay, aren't you? About me buying Star, I mean?'

'Of course. Why wouldn't I be?'

'Okay. Good.'

'It was a really lovely gesture – showing your appreciation for the people you care most about.'

'Yeah – that's the way I see it.'

'Good.' Then she kisses me and turns out the bedside light.

* * *

Before we know it, we're back on the aeroplane heading home. Rain lashes against the small porthole window as we begin our descent.

'Thanks for a super birthday', says Rita, as we fasten our seatbelts. 'I've enjoyed it, having you all to myself.'

'Thank *you,*' I say, kissing the top of her head. 'We'll always have Rome.'

'Yes, we will.'

5

★ DES JAMES ★

I'm sat in the living room in my favourite chair, staring at the telephone. *Just pick it up and ring her.* Instead, I walk to the kitchen and fetch a can of lager. I sit down again and my gaze returns to the telephone. I crack open the can and take a sip. *What's the worst thing she can say? Why have you left things so long, dad?*

I pick up the receiver and punch in her number. I'm connected. I bite my lip nervously. She picks up.

'Hello, Marsha speaking'.

I hesitate before answering. 'Marsha. It's me.'

'Dad.'

The line goes quiet. I press on. 'How's things, Birmingham way?' I say.

'Oh, you know – let's just say I'm pleased it's Friday.'

That voice. Just like her mother's. 'Busy week?'

'Yeah, you could say that.'

'How's Kyle?' I say.

'Kyle is – well … he's fine.'

A short silence follows. 'Er, I was just wondering if the pair of you would like to come up to Nottingham sometime?'

'Er, yeah. That'd be great.'

'I thought of making a Bajan fish stew. How about a week on Saturday?'

'Kyle is at Del's that week, dad.'

'That's a pity,' I say. 'But you're still welcome. Then the three of us could make a point of all getting together the time after that?'

There's a momentary silence. 'Okay. That's a date, then.' She hesitates briefly before continuing. 'How have you been, Dad?'

'Alright, love. You know. Better than I have been for some time. I'll tell you more about that when I see you.'

* * *

I stir the contents of the pan. I add the coconut milk and red pepper. As the contents comes to the boil the aroma hits me, transporting me back to the tiny kitchen of my parents' home on the outskirts of Bridgetown, Barbados.

Marsha appears in the kitchen doorway. 'I put the flowers on the chest of draws in the front room,' she says.

'All right love. Thank you.'

'Is there anything I can do?'

'You can fetch me a bottle of lager from the fridge if you like – oh and while you're at it, bring me the marinated fish mixture. It's on the middle shelf. I'll need to add that any minute.'

* * *

Ten minutes later we're sat together in the living room eating and drinking.

'This is delicious - just like how mum's used to taste.'

I take a swig of lager and smile. 'Now that *is* a compliment!' I say. I call out towards the living room, where the cask containing Shirelle's ashes are standing on the mantlepiece.

'Did you hear that Shirelle, love?'

Marsha bursts into laughter. 'Dad!'

'What?' I say, smiling. 'I talk to her all the time!'

Marsha smiles at me and takes a sip of wine. 'I'll never forget the first time I tasted Bajan fish stew. I was around eight or nine.'

'You'd just turned eight,' I say. 'I remember because it was the first time you asked your mum and I how it was that you were both black *and* British.' Marsha smiles and takes a sip of wine. I look out of the window. 'You were so interested, you know, when we told you about us growing up in Barbados. It was a great place to live – paradise on earth – until Hurricane Janet changed everything. The only upside about leaving was that me and your mum got to start over again here while we were both still young. Fast forward a few months and I was working on the buses, driving people to and from the Arndale Centre!'

'Talk about culture shock,' says Marsha.

I smile. 'From Bridgetown to Beeston. Things couldn't have been more different. But we adapted. We *had* to. And then in '59 you came along.' I send her a smile. Marsha smiles too and looks down at her hands in her lap. 'We'd moved twice within Nottingham by then.' I place my knife and fork on my empty plate and dab my mouth with my napkin. 'I've now lived longer in Nottingham than I did in Bridgetown. For all its faults, Nottingham ain't so bad.'

* * *

After clearing the table, we move into the living room. Despite my sentiments about Nottingham, the room's interior is a cluttered shrine to my birthplace. The walls are decorated with framed photographs and colourful prints of Old Bridgetown – and a multi-coloured wall hanging covers most of the far wall. A pair of Barbadian indoor plants, which are threatening to take over the far corner of the room, complete the effect. I take a seat in my favourite armchair. On her way over, Marsha notices something lying on the living room table. She picks it up and holds it up to me.

'What's this, dad?'

'Oh yeah. I left it out to show you. I've become a part-owner in a racehorse.'

'Get away!'

'I know.'

'How come?'

'Through a friend of mine. A fella from the bookies. His name is Andy. Last year he came into a lot of money, so he bought a horse for a few of us to own together. There's nine of us in all. We formed a syndicate and everyone owns an equal share.'

'Wow! Have you seen him run yet?'

'"He" is actually a "she". Manvers Road Star is her name, or "Star" for short. Yes, we saw her run back in January. She didn't win, but our trainer is targeting a race for her at Colwick Park, Nottingham's local track.'

'When is she going to run?'

'Sometime in May.' My eyes become watery. Marsha notices.

'What is it?' she says.

'No, it's nothing. I'm being silly. It's just that it's really helped, you know? Since Andy bought that horse, she's been the perfect distraction, you know - from missing your mum - given me something else to think about.'

Marsha sits down beside me. She gives me a hug. 'I know how much you miss her, dad. I do too.'

'I know you do, love.'

'Sorry. I'm being soft.'

Marsha looks at me. 'No, you're not.'

'It's funny,' I say. 'Since Star came along, I've not felt the need for the church so much either. Do you think that's wrong?'

'No.'

'It's just I saw the pastor the other day on my way to Morrisons. From the way he looked at me, he must think that he's lost me to the Presbyterians!' I burst into laughter. Marsha joins in. A short silence falls over us.

'So,' I say. 'How's things with Kyle?'

'Oh, you know. He has his ups and downs. I love him to bits but he can seem so remote sometimes.'

'Isn't that his age?'

'Possibly.' An anxious expression sweeps across Marsha's face. 'He has his GCSEs this year.'

'Blimey. Where does the time go?'

'I know,' says Marsha. 'This past year, his teachers have told me that he's been experiencing some difficulties.'

'What kind of difficulties?'

'Social difficulties. Getting along with his classmates, integrating generally. The teachers all agree that he's bright – it's just that he has difficulty showing it when it counts, you know, in exams. He's been seeing a child psychologist.' Marsha hesitates. 'They think he may have some kind of disorder.'

'Like things aren't hard enough for a black kid of his age.' I take a swig of lager. I think for a moment. 'Perhaps I could come down? Take him to see Villa play? Or is he a Bluenose? I know. Does he like fishing?'

Marsha smiles. 'He's not really into football, dad. He loves his music though. I think he's been at Del's record collection, as it's mainly old stuff at the moment: Curtis Mayfield, Gil Scott-Heron.' I smile. 'And he's good with technical things – you know, finding out how stuff works. I'm trying to get him to apply to technical college. Everything sort of hinges on his exam results. Oh, and animals. He loves animals.'

'Does he?'

'Yeah. I was thinking about it the other day, how he's always been really good with the pets he's had. And he reads books about animals of all kinds.'

'That's good.'

Marsha nods. 'I just wish the kids in his class saw it that way.' She pauses for a moment before continuing. 'Del and I meet his psychologist once a month. She says that teenagers with the kind of difficulties Kyle has benefit a lot from owning a pet. It's because the love animals show their owners is unconditional. Anyway, last month I brought this up with him - whether he was interested in getting a new one?'

'What did he say?'

'He said he'd think about it.' A short silence falls over the room. 'Do you remember Brian, his rabbit?' Marsha says, smiling.

I take a swig of lager. 'I do! How he loved that rabbit!'

'He did. He worshipped him!' she says.

I see Marsha's empty glass. 'Would you like a top-up?' I say.

'Thanks dad, but I'm driving. Water is fine. I'll fetch it.'

'Don't be daft. I'm not that decrepit.' Marsha laughs. I

fetch a glass of water from the kitchen. 'How does he get along with his dad?'

'I'm not sure. According to Del, they clash a bit – about homework, about Kyle not keeping his bedroom tidy. Del does try - and Kyle has become very particular about his food. I think that might be part of his … condition.' She looks at her watch. 'Dad, I'll need to get going soon. But before I do, can we take a look through your old photo album together?'

'Of course,' I reply. 'What brought that on?'

'I don't know. The fish stew, perhaps?'

* * *

I walk across the room to a large chest of drawers. I slide it open. Inside are two photo albums, one on top of the other. The one on top has a red cover and the one underneath it has a blue one. I pick up the top one. Marsha moves to the sofa and I sit down beside her, placing the album down in front of us on my cluttered coffee table. She opens it and slowly starts turning the pages. She stops and points at a studio portrait. It's a black and white photograph which has been hand-tinted using watercolours.

'Your and mum's wedding portrait.'

'That's right,' I say. 'I hired that suit. You can tell, as it looks a bit big for me.' A couple of pages later, she comes upon some pictures from our wedding reception.

'Where was it held again? It looks so fancy?'

'At Garrison Savannah racecourse in one of their suites.'

'That's right,' she says.

'Your mum worked there as a waitress on race days and for other private functions. It meant we could hire the room at a special rate.'

'Didn't you work there too?'

'Yeah, but not in hospitality.'

'But it's where you and mum met first met?'

'It is.'

Marsha turns to the next page and smiles. 'This has to be my all-time favourite photograph of you both.'

I take a look. Shirelle and I are sat beside one another on a beach smiling into the camera. In the background, a distinctive yellow pier juts out into the ocean. The sea is so blue, it's hard to tell where the sea becomes the sky. 'Ah - Pebbles Beach,' I sigh.

'It's such a pretty name,' Marsha says.

'Yes. After your mum and I began courting, it became our favourite spot in all of Barbados.'

'I can see why. It's beautiful.'

I nod. 'It's close to the racecourse, see. As soon as your mum got off work, we would wander down there together.' I hover my index finger over the photograph and point. 'Look. Beyond us, in the ocean. What do you see?'

She looks closer. 'Wow. Are they horses?'

'Yes. After the last race, some of the grooms would walk them down to the beach and bathe them in the ocean. It was one such groom who we asked to take this picture.'

'Cool.'

'We had a routine whenever we visited the beach. I'd buy us ice cold sodas or a couple of beers from a vendor near the seafront. Meanwhile, your mum would take off her shoes and walk barefoot towards the sea. Once I caught her up, we would sit down in the sand with our drinks and talk. Sometimes we talked for hours, joking together, laughing.' Marsha turns to me and kisses me on the cheek. 'What was that for?' I say. She just smiles at me and continues to turn the pages, scanning each photograph with interest. A few pages on she says, 'Oh, this one I remember!' The photograph shows Shirelle holding Marsha in her arms, a frilly beige bonnet framing her cherubic face.

'I took that in our garden when we lived in Forest Fields,' I say. 'Your first summer. The weather was glorious. You've not changed at all!' I laugh. Marsha joins in. The next photograph is a flash-lit colour one. It shows Marsha, Shirelle and myself sat under a bright red sun parasol emblazoned with the Martini logo, seated in an outdoor restaurant.

'Look at us!' says Marsha.

'Yes - now that is a "milestone" photograph if there ever was one. Read out the caption,' I say.

'"The James Family first holiday abroad. Marbella, August, 1967."'

'To be honest, it couldn't have been more different to the tranquillity of Pebbles Beach, but it was special all the same. Holidaying abroad was still something quite new in those days. Not like today.'

'Going by the year, I'd just turned seven,' says Marsha. I smile and nod. She looks at the clock on the living room wall. Slowly she closes the photo album and leans back on the sofa. 'I ought to make tracks.' For a moment I become quiet. Marsha detects it. 'What is it?' she says.

'I guess looking through those old photographs of Barbados, brought up something I regret.'

'What's that?'

'That your mum and I never got to show you the place.'

'Don't be silly,' says Marsha.

'We always intended to.'

'Dad, stop it.'

'I regret it, that's all. Some other expense would always come along. The oven would need replacing, our fridge would break down. The last time we came very close to going was in 1991. Kyle was about to turn nine, shortly after your mum got ill. But that's another story.'

* * *

I'm stood on the kerb outside the house. Marsha is searching in her handbag for her car keys. After finding them, she says, 'thanks for a super evening, dad.'

'You too. Next time, the three of us can meet up. If Kyle would like to, that is.' I give her a tight squeeze. She opens the car door and gets in. 'Drive carefully, love,' I say, leaning my hand on the roof of the car. She winds the window down and smiles her big smile. I see Shirelle in her expression. Then with a toot of the horn, she's gone.

6

★ ANDY ★

Star's third race comes at the beginning of April. Following two runs racing left-handed, Ray decides to throw a right-handed run into the mix. For this purpose, he makes entries for races at Beverley, Leicester, Kempton Park and Salisbury. I'm at home enjoying a bottle of duty-free wine with Rita when he rings at the forty-eight hours declaration stage.

'Hi Ray, how's Star?'

'She's well. Rested, happy in herself and back in light work. Just to tell you that having checked the weather forecast, I'm leaning towards Kempton.'

'Okay.'

'I know how keen you all were on a day trip to Leicester, but Kempton is the only course with soft in the description, see?'

By now I was fully averse to approving conditions that would suit Star the least. 'Then Kempton it is.'

* * *

I miss Star's run because of work – but meet up with Des at Manvers Road bookies early evening to watch a re-run. The shop is almost empty so Glen joins us, looking on from behind the thick Perspex screen. I sit on a stool beside Des.

'A torrential downpour changed the going to heavy shortly before the race. Right Andy', he says, pointing at the screen, 'here goes.' Des, Glen and I follow the re-run. Star breaks well but approaching the turn is soon back pedalling. 'Look - she's pulling left, Callum is tugging right, see?' he says. I nod. One furlong from home and the field is strung out like washing. A voice rings out from the other end of the counter.

'Oi, Glen! You gonner take this bet, or what?' Glen scurries back to his till, just as the race ends. As the highlights from Kempton Park continue, something strikes me. Des notices. 'What is it?' he says.

'It's probably nothing', I say, stubbing out my cigarette. 'I just hope we haven't already put Star off already, you know?'

'How do you mean?'

'Racing,' I say. Getting beaten out of sight three times can't be doing much for her confidence?'

'I know what you mean. I guess we won't really know till next time, eh?'

'True. Colwick Park – "the big one."'

* * *

I'm at home when the telephone rings. It's Ray.

'Just to let you know that I've contacted with the British Horse Racing Authority about getting Star rated for handicaps. It will take a few weeks, but the process is now underway.'

'That's great, Ray.'

'She was a bit stiff after Kempton, so we've turned her out in the paddock, where she's relaxing and enjoying life. So, Colwick Park next.'

'Bloody hell, yeah - this is really happening.'

'It is, Andy. By the way, I've taken a look at the fixture list. It's six weeks until their first meeting of the season. Their second one is ten days after that which is great, as it gives us a bit of leeway, you know, as regards her fitness and at which of the two meetings to run her.'

'Good to know.'

'When I hear back from the handicapper, you'll be the first to hear about it.'

'Okay, Ray,' I say. 'Er, in the meantime, would you mind if I come up to the stable to see her every once and a while?'

'Of course not. Just give me a couple of days' notice.'

'All right. How about a day next week? Tuesday would be ideal as it's my day off.'

'That shouldn't be a problem. Let me just check the training roster.' The line goes momentarily quiet, before he returns on the line. 'You're in luck. Star will be out in the third lot, so be up here for eight, yeah?'

* * *

I pull into Nine Elms Stables. A blanket of mist hangs low in the sky, as I head towards the stone cottage. The front door is open so I enter. Stepping into the hall way, I find a half-opened door to my immediate left. The words 'Racing Office' are displayed on a shiny brass plaque on the middle of it. Nudging the door open, I find Ray and Ellie sitting opposite one another at Rays messy desk, drinking coffee.

'Good morning. You found us then?' says Ray. 'Welcome to the nerve-centre of my training operation. Fancy a cuppa?'

'Yes please. A black coffee, with two sugars,' I say, pulling up a chair. Ray returns with my coffee in a chipped mug, sits himself back at his desk and looks at me.

'This morning, Ellie will work Star alone on the six-furlong grass straight. She's in light work at the moment, so she'll be doing little more than a canter.'

'No stopwatch required today, then?' I joke.

Ray laughs. 'No, but you may want to borrow these?'

He passes me a pair of battered binoculars. I drain my coffee and take them. 'Thank you.'

'Okay then', says Ray, getting to his feet. 'Back to work.'

* * *

The three of us set off in the direction of the stabling area. The clip-clop of hooves follows us, as string of newly exercised horses pass by, their coats glistening with sweat. I walk beside Ellie. Up ahead, Ray studies each passing horse with an eagle eye. He stops a handsome bay and asks his work rider some questions, as Ellie and I pass on by.

Ellie and I make small talk on the way to meet Star. 'So are you the latest in a long line of McGovern's working in racing?' I say.

She laughs. 'No, not at all. My dad is on the board of the Bank of Ireland and my mum's an economist. We don't really have much contact.'

'Sorry to hear that.'

'It's fine. Ironically, it was through my dad's job that I first got interested in becoming a jockey. The Bank of Ireland are big sponsors of racing back home and though dad has little interest in the sport – hurling is his thing – he enjoys the hospitality side of things. Consequently, as a kid, I was taken along to all the big meetings. Leopardstown, the Curragh, Galway - you name it.'

'Cool.'

'I started out with pony racing when I was eight and it went on from there.'

'Were your parents supportive?'

'Yes, at first, but I think they just thought I'd grow out of it. I didn't though. Things came to a head at the end of my first year of uni when they found out I'd spent most of the year riding out for different trainers on the Curragh rather than studying!' Ellie laughs. I join in. 'I dropped out of uni and that was that really. Dad went ballistic. I'm not sure he's ever really forgiven me.'

'Respect for sticking with what you love. That was bold.'

Ellie laughs. 'I moved out of my folks' place and began riding out full time, even though some of the trainers I rode out for warned me I was too tall to become a professional jockey.'

'How tall are you? I say.

'Five foot six – four inches above the ideal height.'

'It didn't stop Richard Hughes, did it?' I quip.

'That's what I told them! Funny you mention him. He's my hero, as well as a fellow Dubliner.' Ellie pauses briefly. 'I think the real reason some of those trainers commented on my height was because secretly they preferred taking on male work riders. Some stuck by me, but in the end, there were more opportunities here in England, which is how I wound up here.'

We continue past a long row of horseboxes. The stabling area is a hive of activity. The more curious horses poke their heads over their stable doors as we pass. Arriving at Star's box, Ellie makes a shrill whistling sound. Star appears at her door. I tilt my head towards her and gently ruffle her mane.

She leans her head in towards me, nudging her head against mine. Ellie looks on. 'She recognises you all right', she says.

'Does she?' I say. Ellie nods. I look into Star's big, mysterious eyes. I hold my fingers to her mouth and she nibbles them. Star blows hard. Ellie laughs softly. 'She's saying good morning'.

'Really?'

'Yeah.'

'Good morning, Star.' I smile and kiss the top of the white blaze below her eyes.

* * *

Ellie, Star and I leave the stabling area. We stop in front of a wooden structure at the foot of the gallops. A short, rickety stairway leads up the side of it to a small, open viewing platform.

'This is your stop', says Ellie. 'See you later.'

I nod. While Ellie canters Star up the six-furlong gallop, I climb the stairway with Ray's binoculars dangling from the strap around my shoulder. I track them through the binoculars as they race back in my direction, dipping in and out of the low-lying mist. It's a magical sight.

* * *

The following Tuesday, Des joins me on the wooden watch tower. We must really look the part; me with my borrowed binoculars from Ray and Des, who has brought his own pair with him.

'Nice bins', I say.

'Thanks. Carl-Zeiss lenses, see?' Des holds them out towards me.

'Proper vintage ones,' I say. 'Cool.'

'Yeah. They were a present from someone when I left Barbados.'

'Nice.' Des and I stand poised at the edge of the tower, binoculars raised, as Ellie and Star set off. It's a bright April morning and visibility is good.

'Ellie has good hands,' says Des.

I watch her as they race by. All I see is a girl riding a horse. 'What do you mean by "good hands?"'

'Ellie shows an unforced communication to Star, via the reins. That Callum is good, but Ellie is better. She's a natural.'

I turn and look at Des. He notices. 'What?'

'Nothing. I just wish I saw half as much as you do.'

Des smiles, a little self-consciously. Ellie addresses us from the foot of the wooden tower.

'That's her lot for today, guys,' she says.

7

★ ANDY ★

Rita and I have a new thing: a watered-down version of our New Year's Day resolutions, made as we lay in bed, nursing hangovers on the first morning of 1997.

'We need to start taking better care of our bodies', she says.

'I agree.'

'Why don't we join a gym?'

'Gyms have never been my thing.'

'Okay,' says Rita. 'How about we go jogging a couple of times a week then?'

'I think I prefer the gym idea', I say, laughing.

She turns to face me. 'You're not really helping, Cooper.'

'I know. What about swimming?'

'You don't like gyms, I hate the smell of chlorine. Any other suggestions?'

I raise myself so I'm sitting up on the edge of the bed. 'I know. How about we take a long walk every weekend?'

'Ending up at a nice pub somewhere?'

'You're on,' I say.

* * *

The Sunday after visiting Nine Elms Stables with Des, Rita and I are out on one such walk. I suggested the grounds of Colwick Country Park. We cycle there on our new mountain bikes, which I treated us to after committing to our new health regime. We padlock them in the Country Park car park, which is also the starting point for the designated three and a half miles walk.

'"Early spring is a perfect time of year to visit"', I say, reading from a pamphlet Rita picked up from the local library. '"A vast woodland area, rich in wildlife that includes dragonflies, butterflies and migratory birds."'

'I believe there's a racecourse here somewhere, too?' Rita says all deadpan.

I smile. 'Which is why I suggest a visit to the aptly named Starting Gate pub when we're done.'

'I was waiting for the racing link,' she says. 'You've got a one-track mind, do you know that?'

'We can go somewhere else if you want? I just thought it might be a good omen for May, that's all?' I say, a little defensively.

'It's fine, Andy. I tell you what, if the food is good, you can take me there again after Star wins her race.'

* * *

An hour or so later, our walk completed, we're back on our bikes. I see the pub sign up ahead. We hobble into the beer garden, just as sun comes out from behind the clouds.

'Okay. You find us a table and I'll get the drinks in,' I say.

A few minutes later, I return to the beer garden. Rita

waves me over. She is in the process of putting up the sun parasol at our table.

'There you go. One rum and coke with ice and two menus.'

'Thank you.' For a moment we just sit there enjoying our drinks. I split open a packet of crisps for us to nibble on.

'Oh yeah, I've been meaning to ask,' she says. 'Is Tuesday your day off next week?'

'It is,' I say, taking a slurp from my pint.

'I've taken the afternoon off, you see. I thought maybe we could do something together?'

'Okay – er …'

'What?'

'No, it's just I was planning on going up to Nine Elms Stables to watch Star train.'

'Oh right.' Rita takes a sip of her drink and nibbles a crisp. 'Didn't you go up there last Tuesday?' she says, opening her menu. 'And the Tuesday before that, if I'm not mistaken.'

'I 'spose I did, yeah - I didn't realise you were keeping count?'

'I'm not - but couldn't you go up there another day this week instead?'

I think for a moment. 'When we were in Rome, I asked if you were all right about me buying Star.'

'I was. I am,' she says.

'Then what is it?'

'Well, I guess I wasn't aware that after returning to Nottingham you were planning on spending all of your spare time visiting her!'

'C'mon, don't exaggerate. Can't we do something together at the weekend instead?'

Her voice steps up a notch. 'So, you're prioritising Star ahead of me?'

'Don't put words in my mouth. You're being ridiculous!'

Rita snaps back. 'Who's the one being ridiculous?'

The girl from behind the bar sidles up to our table. 'Are you ready to order?'

'The veggie burger please, with salad and fries', Rita says curtly.

'I'll take the gourmet burger.'

'Salad and fries?'

'Yes please.'

Silence falls over our table. It continues after our food arrives. I can't put into words how I am feeling because my thoughts are all jumbled up. Instead, I just munch my burger in silence and avoid eye contact. Eventually we finish our food and cycle back to Sneinton – and when I ask, Rita declines coming up to the flat.

* * *

Early evening, I wander up to St Nicholas' church cemetery. It's my first visit since dad died last autumn. On my way, I pick up two bouquets from the forecourt of the all-night garage. I sit at my usual bench along the stony pathway, just a few yards from their gravestones. I light a cigarette and as I smoke it, recall the countless visits I made up here to sit in mum's presence, after dad and I fell out. The light is beginning to fade, so I make my way over. I brush away the dead leaves and debris lying on their graves, and lay the fresh flowers in their place. I gently kiss the top of mum's headstone and then lay my hand on dad's, newer one. The stone is cold against my hand. 'Thank god we made our peace dad, before it became too late,' I say under my breath. A tear rolls down my cheek. I brush it away. ‘I just can’t help wishing though, you know - wishing we’d had more time together before you …’ My words tail off. Out of the corner of my eye, I see the church warder locking the main doors to the church. There’s a chill in the air. I turn my jacket collar up against the cold. Then I return to the stony pathway, turn left and make my way home.

8

★ ANDY ★

It's the evening after our weird visit to the Starting Gate pub. I'm stood on the door step outside Rita's flat. I ring the bell and a moment later she opens the door. 'Hi. These are for you.' I hold out a bouquet of flowers.

Rita stands before me dressed in leggings and a baggy white t-shirt. Her hair is down around her shoulders. 'Thank you', she says, taking them. 'Do you want to come in?' I nod and follow her along her narrow hallway. 'Something to drink?' she says.

'Have you got any beer?'

'Go through to the living room. I'll bring one in.'

I enter Rita's small living room. A half-finished glass of red wine is standing on the table, next to a copy of the Nottingham Evening Post. I sit down. Rita joins me and hands me a glass of lager.

'Thanks.' I take a mouthful. 'So, I had a bit of a think last night.' I look down at my hands in my lap. 'You're right – I could have talked to you before making plans for my day off this week. So, if your offer of doing something together tomorrow still stands, then I'm up for it.'

She takes a sip of wine. 'That depends.'

'Depends on what?'

'On whether you *want* to spend the afternoon with me?'

'Of course, I do.'

'Are you sure?'

'C'mon', I say.

Rita smiles. 'Then I have a suggestion. Why not ring Ray and ask if we can visit Star together at the weekend? Then tomorrow, I thought maybe we could catch a film? What do you reckon?'

I smile. 'That would be great. What's on?'

Rita picks up her Nottingham Evening Post and turns to the 'what's on' pages. Good Will Hunting, As Good as It Gets and The Full Monty?' she says.

'What do you want to see?'

'No. You choose,' she says.

'How about The Full Monty?'

'The Full Monty it is then.'

A short silence follows. 'I'm really pleased you want to come and see Star with me', I say.

'Don't sound so surprised. You've never actually asked me before.'

'Haven't I?'

'No.'

* * *

The following morning, I ring Ray and ask about delaying my visit until Sunday instead.

'No problem. It's funny, as I was just about to ring you. Yesterday afternoon I heard back from the racing authorities. Star has been allocated an opening mark of sixty.'

'Is that good?'

'Well, we'll know more on Sunday when I run her against a seventy-five rated horse. But yes, I'm optimistic.'

* * *

That afternoon, Rita and I have a great time at the cinema and after a drink at a pub opposite the Odeon, we walk back to the flat via Hockley, where I stop in my tracks outside a restaurant.

'The Bombay Lime', says Rita.

'Yes - the scene of our first date.'

Rita peers through the smoked glass frontage. 'What a shame it's so busy.'

'Yeah', I say. 'Unless you've already made a reservation.'

She beams at me. 'You haven't, have you?'

I smile and opening the door for her, add, 'I do have my romantic moments you know.'

* * *

Back at my place later, lying next to one another in bed, Rita turns towards me and kisses me good night. 'Back to work tomorrow,' she says. 'Give me a nudge before you leave, yeah?'

'Sure. And thanks for a great day'.

'You too. It was fun, wasn't it? Good night then.'

'Yeah, good night.'

Rita turns out the light and rests her hand on my chest. I lay there staring up at the ceiling in the dark. 'Can I ask you something?' I say.

'Sure.'

'Do I make you happy?'

Rita turns the light back on. 'Where did that come from?'

'I don't know. I just wondered.'

'Sometimes,' she giggles. I pinch her in the darkness. 'Of course, you do', she says.

'Good. It's just, well - I've never felt happier with anyone, that's all. And I just thought you should know.'

Rita looks me in the eyes. 'Thank you.'

'You're welcome,' I say. A short silence follows. 'They're not always easy, are they?'

'What aren't?' says Rita.

'Relationships.'

'No, they're not. They need working on. But if both people believe in making it work, then it will.' She turns the light out again.

Lying there in the darkness, I think about Rita's words and realise that she's right. 'Goodnight,' I say.

'Goodnight, Andy.'

'I love you,' I say softly.

'I love you too,' she says and turns around towards me.

9

★ DES ★

'All right, Des?'

'Not bad youth and you?' I walk in to the kitchen with the handheld phone, just as two slices of bread jump out of the toaster.

'Yeah, all good,' says Andy. 'Rita and I just wondered if you'd like to see Star train tomorrow?'

'Sure. What time?'

'How about we pick you up around eight?'

'Perfect. Look forward to it! See you then.'

I eat my toast and start filling out a placepot slip. Within five minutes it's done. I turn off the TV and gather together my other betting slips. Just as I am about to set off to the bookies, the phone rings again.

'Dad, it's me.'

'Hi Marsha. How's things?'

The line goes quiet for a moment. 'I don't know. Kyle has just turned up. He's all upset, saying he doesn't want to live at his dad's anymore.'

'Oh.'

'I need to talk to him.'

'Of course.'

'I've rung Del already. He's going to come round later after he gets off work. Thing is, I don't think Kyle should be here too as it could get too, well, volatile.'

'Yes, I see.'

'Dad, do you have any plans for tonight?'

'Nothing concrete. Why?'

'I just wondered if you could put him up over night? I'm sorry it's such short notice.'

'Of course. I've been hoping to spend some time with him anyway.'

Marsha sighs with relief. 'Thank you, Dad. I'm going to sit down with him now and try to get him to talk to me. Afterwards, I thought we might do something nice together in town.'

'That sounds like a good idea. Just call me later when you know what time he'll be arriving at the station.'

'Will do - and thanks again.'

'You're welcome.'

I ring off - and ring Andy to opt out of tomorrow's trip.

* * *

Later that afternoon, I take the bus into town. I meet Kyle from the 17.14 from Birmingham New Street. It's few minutes delayed, so I wait at the end of the platform. Five minutes later, the train pulls into the station. Though it's been a couple of years, I recognise Kyle right away. He has a wiry frame and is no taller than his mum. He's wearing jeans, a pair of adidas trainers and a lightweight jacket, zipped up to the top. On his back is a rucksack. A pair of head phones straddle his round head, on top of which sits a back-to-front Metz baseball cap. When he sees me, he mimes: 'wait', before switching off his music.

'Hi Kyle,' I say brightly.

'Hello, Grandpa.'

I step forward to embrace him. He appears uncomfortable, so I rub his right shoulder instead.

* * *

Half an hour later I unlock the front door to the house and help him off with his rucksack.

'Make yourself at home. Can I get you something to drink?'

'Have you got any Fanta?'

'I do. Got some in especially,' I say.

'Great.'

I return to the living room with a can of Fanta and a bottle of Heineken. I find Kyle sitting at the living room table, grappling with my old transistor radio which I left out for him.

'This thing's' ancient.'

'I know', I say. 'I like to listen to the cricket on it. But last time I tried, I couldn't get it to work.'

Kyle looks up. 'I can have a go at fixing it if you like?'

'That would be great.'

He takes a mouthful of Fanta and gets to work.

'Your mum rang this morning. She gave me some tips about what food you like?'

'Oh right.'

'I thought I'd do us fishfingers, baked beans and a fried egg, later? Sound alright?'

Kyle nods.

'Good.'

He takes his eyes off the transistor radio and tilts his head towards me. 'Er, when you do it, can you make sure that nothing touches each other on the plate?'

'Sure.' I say. 'Maybe when everything is ready, you can join me in the kitchen and show me how you mean?' Kyle has already returned his attention to my transistor radio, unscrewing the back of it with a screwdriver from the tool box I left on the table. 'Kyle?'

'Hum? Yeah, sure,' he says.

* * *

Kyle and I are sitting at my kitchen table eating. The fishfingers, baked beans and eggs sit in splendid isolation on different parts of our plates. 'Your mum said you had a bit of a barny with your dad?'

He looks up at me. 'I don't want to talk about it,' he mumbles.

'Alright,' I say, cutting a fishfinger in two.

A short silence falls between us. 'Dad thinks I'm difficult,' Kyle says eventually.

'How do you mean?'

'When it comes to homework and stuff.'

'Right.'

'It just that it takes me time to get it finished. I get distracted.'

'I see.'

And then there's my bedroom.'

'What about it?' I say.

'He's always on at me about how I don't keep it tidy.'

'Now there I sympathise a bit with Del, Kyle.'

I look up from my food. Kyle is pushing a fishfinger around his plate with his fork.

'The thing is, his room is untidier than mine. He doesn't like it when I bring *that* up!'

I try hard not to smile but Kyle catches my eye. He reciprocates.

'Anything else bothering you at the moment?' I say.

Yeah. School.'

I take a swig of lager. 'In what way?'

'I don't like it.'

'What in particular don't you like?'

'Everything. My class mates, everyone.'

'Why's that, Kyle?'

'Because I never know when anyone is being serious with me or when they are joking.'

'That must be difficult.'

'Yeah. It is. It's confusing. And it gets me in to trouble.'

'But I guess you have a couple of mates, yeah?' I say. Kyle shrugs his shoulders. Something tugs hard on my heart strings. 'Okay, sunshine', I say. 'How about I take care of these plates, while you get back to my transistor radio?'

Kyle nods. 'Sure. Er. Thanks for Tea.'

* * *

That evening, we're sat together watching a film. Kyle continues to plug on with my radio at the same time. During the commercial break, an idea comes to me.

'Kyle, do you like horses?'

'Horses?'

Yeah. Racehorses. I own a share in one.'

He looks at me. 'What, like a thoroughbred?'

'Yeah. A thoroughbred.'

'What's his name?'

'Manvers Road Star. He's a "she" actually.'

'A filly?'

Yeah, that's right. A filly.'

'Yeah, I like them - though I've never actually seen one in real life. Only on the telly, you know – when dad has the racing on. He usually shouts at the one he's put money on to run faster.'

'Right,' I say, with a knowing smile.

Kyle returns his attention to my radio. A moment or so later, he screws on the back, rotates the volume dial and presses the 'on' button. There follows a crackling sound and all of a sudden, a Madonna song is blaring out over the airwaves. Kyle beams. I beam back at him and hold up my hand. Kyle does the same and I 'high-five' him. 'Thank you.' I take out my wallet and remove a five-pound note. 'For your troubles.' I hand him the money.

'Thanks.'

I think for a moment. 'Do you have like a careers adviser at school?'

'Yeah. Mr Woods.'

'Have you met with him?' Kyle goes quiet. 'Kyle?'

'Yeah. A couple of times.'

'How did it go?'

'All right. He asked me if I had any ideas for what I want to do after I leave?'

'Okay,' I say. 'And what did you say?'

I told him I might try technical college.'

'That sounds promising. What did he say?'

'He said it all depended on my GCSE results…'

'Right.' A short silence follows. It's me who breaks it. 'I was wondering. How would you like to meet Star tomorrow?'

'Star?'

'Yeah - that's what we call her for short, our filly. I just wondered if you'd like to visit her? You know, at the stable?

Watch her being trained for her next race, before heading back to your mum's?'

Kyle smiles. 'Sure.'

'All right. I just need to make a quick phone call. Check to see if it would be okay.'

* * *

I ring Andy from the kitchen. 'I've had a change of heart about tomorrow. I'd really like to come to see Star with you and Rita after all.'

'Okay. Great, Des.'

'The thing is, my grandson Kyle has come to stay with me at short notice. Would it be all right if he tagged along?'

10

★ ANDY ★

Rita rolls down the passenger door window as I pull in to Des' road.

'There they are,' she says.

Des and his grandson are stood on the curb outside his house. I pull the car over.

Rita rolls down her window. 'Morning, Des', she says brightly.

'Morning Rita', he says.

'You must be Kyle?' Rita says, addressing Des' grandson.

Kyle nods shyly under his Metz cap. 'Hello'.

'Nice to meet you,' says Rita. 'Hop in the back, guys.'

Des opens the back door and he and Kyle climb onto the backseat. I turn around and greet them. I hold out my hand and face Kyle. 'I'm Andy. A friend of your grandpa's.'

Kyle smiles shyly and shakes my hand. Des snaps his seat belt on and after helping Kyle on with his, we get on our way.

* * *

We find Ray and Ellie waiting for us outside the cottage. We exit the car and walk over. As we approach, Ray says, 'Good morning, everyone.'

'Morning Ray,' I say. 'We have a new visitor with us.'

'So I see.'

'This is my grandson, Kyle,' says Des.

'Hi Kyle', says Ray, smiling. They shake hands.

Des continues. 'When I mentioned to Kyle that I had a share in a racehorse, he was really keen to meet her.'

'Horses have among the largest eyes of any land mammal,' says Kyle.

Ray smiles. 'Yes, they do.'

Kyle continues. 'And because their eyes are positioned on the sides of their heads, their range of vision is around three hundred and fifty degrees.'

'You've done your homework,' says Ray, smiling.

Kyle sends Ray a curious look. 'It wasn't homework. Stuff like that just interests me.'

Des and Rita exchange smiles. Ray says, 'they're extraordinary creatures, aren't they, Kyle – horses?' Kyle nods. Then gesturing towards Andy, Rita and Des, Ray says, 'so, how about we go and see Star in action? Kyle doesn't reply, but his eyes twitch excitedly.

* * *

The five of us gather on the roof of the viewing tower. I hand Ray's spare pair of binoculars to Rita and she holds them up to her eyes. Kyle looks on through Des' pair. Two horses and jockeys stand motionless at the three- furlong pole. Ellie and Star and another stable lass on the other horse.

'I've told Ellie to give the other horse a few yards head

start,' says Ray, 'and to try to pull Star upsides by the six-pole.' Ray raises a flag above his head and waves them off. Ellie and Star give the other horse roughly a ten-yard start. One furlong out, Ellie starts to get serious on Star. Within a few strides she has her in full flight and is rapidly closing the gap. With half a furlong to go, Ellie pulls Star upside the lead horse, breezes past and leaves him in their wake. Ellie and Star flash past below us with a two-length lead, going away.

'Wow!' says Kyle.

Des pats Kyle on the shoulder. 'She's quite something, isn't she?'

Kyle returns the smile. 'Yes, she is.'

I turn to Ray. 'Blimey,' I say. 'Does that mean what I think it means?'

Ray smiles. 'It does. That lead horse is called Prairie Falcon. He won off a mark of seventy-five last week.'

'And Star just waltzed past him!' laughs Rita. 'That makes Star around fifteen pounds well in!' Ray looks at Rita and raises an eyebrow.

'Don't look so surprised,' I say. 'Rita used to work at the local bookies to help get herself through uni.'

* * *

Back at the cottage, Ray leads us into to his office and scans his wall calendar. 'Star is on course to run at Colwick in nine days' time,' he announces. I squeeze Rita's hand. She squeezes back. Ray continues. 'I'll give her a nice easy time of it this week, before getting one more run into her next Sunday. Give me a ring if any of you would like to come up and see it.'

'Can we come, Grandpa?' says Kyle.

Des smiles. 'If it's okay with Ray and Andy - and your mum, of course.'

'It's fine by me,' says Ray.

'Me too,' says Andy. Kyle smiles broadly.

11

★ DES ★

I'm watering my wall plants in the living room when the phone rings. I put down the small enamel watering can beside the pot and pick up.

'Just to let you know that Kyle is home safely. Thanks again for putting him up at such short notice.'

I smile down the telephone. 'It was nothing Marsha. Really.'

'He said you've been invited back to see Star next Sunday?'

'That's right.'

'Perhaps he could make a day trip of it, dad?' says Marsha.

'Sure. He seemed to love being up there, you know, around the horses. By the way, did he tell you that he fixed my old transistor radio?'

Marsha laughs. 'He didn't. But it doesn't surprise me.'

'I can listen to the cricket again! By the way, how did your chat with Del go?'

'Good. I told him he needs to be more supportive of Kyle,

particularly now, in his final school year. Del has promised me he'll work with him, not against him.'

I smile down the phone. 'Let me know later in the week what time I should be at the station next Sunday, yeah?'

'Will do, dad. Till then.'

* * *

I replace the telephone receiver and return to watering my plants. When I'm done, I gaze out of the front room window and think about Kyle. I fetch a can of beer from the fridge and walk to the chest of draws. Opening it, I pick up the red photo album Marsha and I recently looked through. I remove the album underneath it, the one with a blue cover. Placing it on the living room table, I open my can of beer and pull up a chair. I sit down and wipe the dust away from the cover, unable to recall the last time I looked through it. Then I take a long, deep breath, open the album and turn to the first page.

12

★ ANDY ★

On my way home after work, I drop by Duke's small solicitors practice on Sneinton Boulevard. He is stood outside having a crafty fag. He smiles as I approach.

'To what do I owe the pleasure?'

We shake hands. 'I have some exciting news about Star. The thing is I want to share it with everyone in person. Can you make it to the King Billy tomorrow evening at around eight?'

'Sounds intriguing,' he says, stubbing out his cigarette. A telephone starts ringing from inside his office. 'Better get that,' he says. 'See you tomorrow evening then.'

'Great, Duke. Till then.'

* * *

Continuing on my way home, I call in to Manvers Road bookies. The Chans are stood with Des, sat at his usual stool, watching the racing, while Big Les is sharing a joke with Glen on the other side of the counter.

'Alright, Andy?' they say in unison.

'Not bad and you?' I say smiling. I place a bet and lose forty quid. I tell everyone about the get together at the King Billy tomorrow evening. Fortunately, everyone can make it. On my way out, I approach Des.

'Alright, Youth?' he says.

'Not bad, Des. Er, has One-Armed been in?' Des shakes his head. 'Not to worry. I'll ring him later,' and with that I leave.

Back at the flat, I ring One-Armed and leave a message with his wife, Colette. Lastly, I call Duke's girlfriend, Ray Baldwin's niece, Laura.

'Ray has entered Star for the six- furlong race at Colwick on Tuesday week.'

'How exciting!' says Laura. 'So, I guess you'd like to take a look at the private hospitality box you've reserved?'

'If that isn't too much trouble?'

'Not at all. Shall we say three o' clock, tomorrow afternoon?'

* * *

Laura and I make small talk as we take the elevator inside Colwick Park grandstand up to the top floor. She takes out a bunch of keys and unlocks private hospitality box number three. We enter. The room is airy and light. Mounted on the walls are various artefacts: a framed black and white print of Further Flight winning Nottingham's listed race for Barry Hills last year, some historical race cards - and a set of bottle-green non-runner plates, arranged in a pattern up one wall.

'I like those,' I say, pointing at the metal plates.

Laura smiles. 'Me too. The groundsman was going to

throw them out. They're from the old results board. I had them cleaned up and hey presto, turned them into artefacts,' she says. She points towards the left-hand side of the room. 'On Tuesday, there'll be a table along this wall set out with food and drink, buffet style.' Pointing to the other side of the room, she says, 'over here will be your private bar – and that flatscreen TV above it the will be showing all the away meetings around the country.'

'Nice', I say. My eyes are drawn to the balcony. Laura notices. 'Why don't you go out and take a look?'

I walk over and open the French-windows. Stepping outside, I take in the view. The racecourse is laid out before me. The sunlit grass is the same shade of green as the pool tables at the Embassy snooker club in town. On the far side of the course adjacent to the one-mile start, I can just make out the roof of Colwick Hall Hotel, poking out above a line of trees. Down below me, there's a perfect view over the finishing line. I imagine us all crammed onto the balcony, cheering Star home. I can barely contain myself.

Laura joins me. 'So, what do you think?'

'It's perfect, Laura. I'll take it.'

* * *

At eight o' clock that evening, Rita and I walk into the King Billy saloon bar and order drinks. Des, Glen, Big Les, Duke, One Armed and the Chan are gathered around a window side table.

'All right everyone?' I pull out a chair for Rita and sit myself beside her. A chorus of greetings echoes around the table.

'So, Andy. What's this news of yours?' says Big Les.

I take a swig of beer and light myself a cigarette. ‘The wait is finally over,’ I say. Silence falls over the table. Seven faces look up at me from their beers. ‘Star is a confirmed runner in the six- furlong handicap at three-thirty in the afternoon at Colwick Park, tomorrow week. The coup is on fellas.’

13

★ ANDY ★

Having been five months in the making, there'd been no shortage of time to devise a plan as to how we could best execute our gamble. And having invited Duke to be a part of this process, the time has arrived for us to share it with the others.

Duke gets the ball rolling. 'On the day of the race, we're going to carry out a double pronged assault on Star's odds. The first part of our plan will be carried out at betting shops in and around Nottingham town centre, shortly before we head off to Colwick Park.' He produces a handful of A5 documents from his jacket pocket. He holds one up to display to everyone. 'As you can see, here is a map of Nottingham, showing the twelve betting shops closest to the city centre. The map is divided into four colour-coded zones, three betting shops per zone.' Duke continues. 'Big Les and I will visit the betting shops in the green zone, Andy and Rita the ones in the blue zone, Des and One-Armed the ones in the yellow zone and the ones in the grey zone are Sammy and Lee's. Now, here is the plan.' He lights one of his miniature cigars. 'Between midday and twelve-thirty, the aim is for each of us to get as many bets on Star as possible. Thirty minutes may sound like plenty of time but in reality, it only allows ten minutes per shop, including the time it will take to get from one shop to the next. This is why we divided the map into four zones, based upon the proximity of the shops to one another.'

'Why are we hitting them at that specific time?' says Sammy.

'Because that is when most betting shop managers will be taking their lunch break', says Duke.

'The more betting shop managers who aren't manning the tills when we pay visit, the bigger our chances of us getting our bets on unquestioned,' I say.

'Smart,' says Big Les.

'Okay guys, some ground rules,' I say. 'No more than a tenner on Star per slip, with a maximum of twenty slips per person. Ten pounds to win, five pounds each way - it's up to each of you how you play things. Unless the field size cuts up dramatically, they should be betting to three places in Star's race. Write Star's race card number on your betting slips rather than her name, so as to avoid arousing unnecessary interest in her.'

Duke continues. 'One way to ensure that your single bets on Star are definitely accepted is to put her in win or each-way doubles with a non-runner – or in patent bets with two non-runners. The rules of bookmaking clearly state that such bets will be settled as the single on Star.'

Sammy pipes up. 'If Star's race is priced up, should we take the odds?'

'Good question, Sammy,' I say. 'With three duck eggs next to her name, I'd be surprised if her early bird price will be shorter than 25/1 – it ought to be 33's or bigger. That said, bookmakers tend to price handicap debutants up cautiously.

Nothing will set the alarm bells ringing more than us lot traipsing around all the bookies in Nottingham taking fancy double figure odds.'

'So,' says Duke, 'erring on the side of caution, just write SP on your slips, or nothing at all.'

'Smart,' says Glen. A murmur of approval swirls around the table.

'One last thing,' I say. 'Mix in a few decoy bets between your singles on Star. This should throw any curious cashiers off the scent. And why not include Star in a few each way Yankees and Lucky Fifteens with other horses you fancy running on Saturday? If Star wins or even places at 33's or bigger and you've combined her with shorties who win, the returns will soon add up.'

'Ditto combination forecast and tricast bets,' says Duke. 'You'll be guaranteed a big dividend with our girl in the mix at long odds, especially if another outsider makes the frame.'

Pat the landlord rings the bell for last orders. This allows us just enough time for Duke and I to go over the second part of our plan – our on-course strategy.

'Ten minutes before Star's race, we'll make our way to the betting ring,' I say.

Duke takes over. 'Upon the nod from Andy, each of us join a queue to a row of bookmakers along the rails. Then a couple of minutes before the off, we strike.'

'From herein,' I say, 'it's each man for himself - the idea being for each of us to get as much money on Star as we can.'

'Remember,' says Duke. 'Bookies along the rails aren't allowed to display their prices. They'll be shouting the odds from their pitches.'

'And Star probably won't get a name check, falling into the "20/1 bar" category,' I say.

'This means we'll have to ask for her odds,' says Duke.

'Depending upon the strength of the market, we shouldn't face too many problems getting some decent bets on an outsider like Star.'

'Most bookies will be keen to balance their books,' I say. 'Get some money in against the favourite and the next two or three in the market.'

A silence falls over the table. Glen is the first to speak. 'You two have really thought this through, haven't you?'

I look at Duke. He looks back at me. We smile at one another and looking at Glen, I realise that we have. To every *minute* detail. Next Tuesday afternoon can't arrive soon enough.

14

★ ANDY ★

The following Sunday at Nine Elms Stables, the viewing tower overlooking the six -furlong gallop is chock-a-block. Des, his grandson Kyle and every syndicate member, with the exception of Rita who is feeling under the weather, is here to witness Star's final blow-out ahead of her race, less than twenty- four hours' away. As Ellie moves Star smoothly through the gears and flashes past beneath us, I swear I feel the tower beneath me creak.

Before everyone piles into the rental van for the journey home, Ray asks for everyone's attention. 'Hand on heart, I couldn't have Star in better shape. The current going at Colwick Park is good, good to firm in places. She won't mind either. There's some showers forecast which, if they arrive, would be perfect. Having been through the form of the opposition, through a line with one of my other horses, you just saw Star run about four pounds clear of the top-rated horse tomorrow. Barring bad luck in running, I cannot see how she will fail to make the first three home. Personally, I think she'll win - so don't be afraid to bet like the men you are!'

* * *

Arriving back in Sneinton early afternoon, I bounce up the stairway to my flat with pound signs in my eyes, turn the key in the door and enter. Rita is laying sprawled out on the sofa in the living room.

'How's Star?' she says. 'How did it go?'

'Brilliantly. She is absolutely primed for tomorrow and looks like a million dollars!'

Rita smiles. I kneel down beside the sofa. 'Are you feeling any better?'

Rita pulls herself up. 'Yeah, well - at least I know now why I felt so off-colour earlier,' she says. She pauses before continuing. 'Andy, I have something to tell you. But before I do, I think you should sit down.' She makes a space on the sofa beside her.

'Okay.' My eyes meet hers, but they're giving nothing away. I sit down and watch her as she takes a deep breath and slowly exhales. Then she looks me in the eyes and says, 'Andy, I'm pregnant. We're going to have a baby!'

PART II

15

★ ANDY ★

I lift Rita off the living room floor and spin her around. She laughs hysterically, slapping me on the back, begging me to stop. Eventually we collapse in a heap on the sofa.

'Can you believe it?' She leans in and kisses me.

'Our very own Mini-Cooper!' I say.

Rita cringes. 'Are you ever serious?'

'I *am* being serious. It's brilliant.' I kiss her. 'You're sure, yeah?'

She smiles. 'One hundred percent. I did a test. Actually, I did two tests. Both positive.'

I hug and kiss her again. 'How long gone are you?'

'Well, I skipped my period in March. After it didn't arrive in April, I've been slowly building up the courage to take a test.'

'When did you last have your period?'

'In the middle of February. Ovulation usually happens two weeks or so after that.'

She smiles as she watches my mind at work.

'Are you thinking what I'm thinking?' I say.

'That our baby could have been conceived in Italy?'

'Exactly!' I think for a moment. 'So how about Claudio for a boy?' I say.

'Or Chiara for a girl?' says Rita smiling.

'That's cute. Or Luigi for a boy?'

Rita laughs. 'Do you really want our son to grow up sounding like a Mafia hood?' I join in her laughter.

'Bella for a girl?' I say.

She puts her arms around my shoulders and kisses me. 'Bella. Now we're getting somewhere.'

* * *

That night, as Rita sleeps peacefully beside me, I start thinking about mum and dad and how happy and proud they'd have felt. I feel a strong pang of regret that they won't be around to meet their grandchild. I kiss Rita in the darkness and try to sleep - but the harder I try, the harder it becomes to rid myself of these thoughts.

* * *

We both spend Monday floating on a cloud. Momentarily, I briefly forget about Star's 'Big Day' tomorrow. After breakfast, we take the bus into town to buy new glad rags to wear to the races. As we make our way across Market Square towards the department stores, Rita links her arm in mine.

'You know that it's just as likely that our baby was conceived right here in good old Nottingham,' I say, as we enter Harringtons outfitters.

'True,' says Rita.

'So, perhaps we ought to consider some traditional British names?'

Rita smiles. 'How about Grace for a girl?'

'I like it,' I say. 'Or James for a boy?' Rita gives me a funny look. 'Okay', I say smiling. 'Well, at least we have until October to decide.'

* * *

I buy myself a stylish two-piece linen suit and a pair of hand-made brown suede brogues. Rita picks a colourful designer summer dress off the rail. She looks stunning, blooming with the early signs of motherhood. By four thirty we're home again. While Rita browses through a baby clothes catalogue at the living room table, I start fretting over tomorrow's race. I go to the kitchen and fetch a beer. Several times I'm close to ringing Ray for an update on Star, but think again. I ring around the boys, instead. One-by-one, I recap on tomorrow's betting shop drill. The last call I make is to Des. 'Remember Des, after you've got as many bets on as you can in your area –'

He cuts me short. 'Head to the taxi-rank on Market Square.'

'Exactly.'

'From where we'll drive up to Colwick Park,' he says.

* * *

One beer later, I join Rita in the living room. 'I think I'll go out for a walk. Do you feel like coming?'

Rita looks up from her magazine. 'Do you mind if I stay put?' she says. I wander over and give her a kiss. She touches my hand. 'Are you feeling nervous?' she says.

'About our baby or about the race?' I say.

'Either,' she says.

'A bit of both, I guess.'

Rita smiles. 'I've just been reading up a little about the pregnancy. Let's not get too carried away, just yet, Andy. Tomorrow I'll ring my GP. She'll allocate me a mid-wife. It won't be until the first ultra-sound that we'll know whether the foetus is healthy or not, so …'

I finish her sentence for her. 'Best keep our news to ourselves for the time being, yeah?'

* * *

Fifteen minutes later, I find myself sat opposite mum and dad's graves. Normally I feel calm up here, at peace, but not today. Something is troubling me, making me feel uneasy. At first, I put it down to tomorrows race, but soon realise that no, it's something else. And that's when the cause of my un-ease appears in my sub-conscious, seven words that fill me with a sudden self- doubt. *Am I really ready to become a dad?*

16

★ ANDY ★

The following morning I'm woken by the sound of the telephone. I look at my alarm clock. It's eight minutes past six. Rita nudges me. I get out of bed and fumble my way into the living room. *So much for a lie on the day of Star's race,* I think to myself.

'All right - for fuck's sake, I'm coming!' I reach the phone and pick up.

'Andy, it's me.'

Coming slowly to my senses, I place the voice. It's Ray.

'Andy?'

'Yeah,' I say, yawning. 'I'm here Ray. What is it?'

'I'm … it's Star.'

'What is it?' The tone of his voice gives him away. Something isn't right.

'Out on my morning rounds, I came by Star's box,' he says.

'Right …'

'I found her lying in the straw, whining with pain. I quickly examined her. It's her right eye.'

My heart starts beating double time. 'What's wrong with it?'

'It's infected. Badly swollen, raw red and …'

'And what, Ray?'

'Oozing a thick yellow discharge.'

I picture Star's beautiful eyes, the first feature I noticed about her. I try to speak but the words don't come.

'I've given her something to reduce the pain and I've phoned my vet. It - it doesn't look good. He'll be here in about half an hour.'

'I'm on my way. I have to see her.' I replace the telephone receiver. *It doesn't look good.* A million thoughts race through my mind.

Rita appears in her dressing gown. 'Who was that? What's going on?'

'It was Ray. Star isn't well.' My eyes fill up. I feel nauseas. 'She's – her eye is inflamed. She … I have to go to the yard. Are you coming?'

* * *

I drive as fast as the speed limit allows. On the journey, I recount to Rita the brief conversation I had with Ray – and when I repeat what he said to describe Star's condition – *'that it doesn't look good'* – a silence falls over us. Rita begins to cry softly beside me. I fight my tears by concentrating on the road ahead. We plummet into our own private thoughts. Five minutes from Edwinstowe the sky darkens, and as I pull the car into the stable it begins to rain. Soon it's a deluge.

We arrive at Star's box wet, cold and fearing the worse. Ray and another man stand in the entrance, as though shielding us from the scene inside. Behind them I catch a glimpse of Star's hind legs. They're motionless, stretched out on her bed of straw. Ray's face is ashen grey. Besides him stands a bespectacled middle-aged man with a large medical bag at his feet.

'This is my vet, Harry,' says Ray. 'He'll bring you up to speed.'

'I've administered her a heavy tranquilizer. She'll be out cold for a couple of hours.' He hesitates before continuing. 'Having examined her eye, as a measure to prevent the spread of further infection, I need your permission to operate.'

'Operate?' I say. Rita squeezes my hand.

'Yes. The formal word is enucleation. In the interest of Star's wellbeing, I have no choice but to recommend removing her right eye.'

I feel faint.

'I'm so sorry, Andy', whispers Ray.

Harry goes on. 'If we leave the eye intact and just ply her with painkillers, the infection goes untreated. That could lead to blindness in both eyes and in the worse-case scenario, prove fatal. On the other hand, if I remove her eye, it will stop the spread of the infection dead. I can perform the operation on the spot, it's quite straight forward. But I can't do anything without your permission.'

A short silence falls over the four of us.

'Ray?' I ask. 'What are the chances of …?' I think again, quickly regaining my moral compass. 'Nothing. Forget it.' Turning to Harry, I say, 'take it out.' I hear Rita whimper.

Harry nods compassionately, picks up his medical bag and turns to Ray. 'Then I'll get on with it.'

As Harry enters Star's box, I say, 'Can I just ask you something? Before you …'

'Of course.'

'Will she be in any pain?'

'No. She won't feel a thing.'

'And afterwards?' asks Rita.

* * *

Ray brews some coffee. When it's ready, he adds a shot of whiskey to his mug. He offers the same to Rita and I. We both nod. Twenty minutes later Harry joins us.

'It's done,' he says from the doorway.

'Will you join us, Harry. Coffee?'

'Yes, thank you.'

Ray holds up the whiskey bottle. Harry declines.

I am now the owner of a one-eyed thoroughbred, I think to myself.

Harry takes a seat beside Ray.

'What next?' I say, numbly.

He glances at his wrist watch. 'She'll regain consciousness mid-morning. Over the next few days, her eye socket will swell up. It will look as though her right eyeball is still there beneath the healing skin. But within days the bulge will go down, leaving a fresh layer of skin, completely covering her right eye socket.'

'What kind of side effects will she be left with?' says Rita.

Harry frowns. 'They'll be both physical and psychological.'

'How do you mean?' I say.

'At first, she'll need to re-learn the simple things again, such as learning to walk in a straight line, balance in general. As the days pass, the biggest challenge for her will be learning to overcome the fear from no longer having any right-sided vision. She'll get easily "spooked" by not being able to see approaching subjects from behind on her right side until very late.' He sighs. 'Quite how she learns to live with these disadvantages depends very much on her own character. Horses are just like people in this regard.'

17

★ ANDY ★

I look up at Ray from my coffee. 'Have you told Ellie about Star yet?'

An anxious expression sweeps across his face. 'Not yet. She's still out with first lot.' He reaches for the telephone on his cluttered desk. 'I need to ring the racing authorities. Declare Star as a non-runner.'

The reality of the situation is quickly sinking in. Once Ray is off the phone, I ask to make a call. He nods and I ring Laura to cancel our hospitality box. The moment I replace the handset, there's a knock on the door.

Ray frowns. 'Excuse me a moment.'

I nod. He heads to the door and opens it slightly, before stepping outside. Rita and I hear two muffled voices from the doorway of the cottage. Suddenly everything goes quiet. The sound of Ellie's voice breaks the silence.

'Noooo! It can't be true!'

I bite my lip. Ellie bursts into the room, her face bright red, her eyes streaming. 'I'm so sorry! Star was fine last night! This is awful!'

Rita and I get out of our chairs and comfort her, just as

Ray re-joins us. He looks on compassionately. 'My yard foreman just messaged me. Star has just regained consciousness.'

* * *

I approach Star's box. She appears out of the darkness from the back. I catch a glimpse of her bandaged right eye. She turns her head to the side and cautiously studies me through her left eye. Slowly I tilt my head towards her, uncertain how she'll react. She moves her head in to meet mine - and when I move my hand to her mouth, my eyes fill up with tears, as she blows through her giant nostrils and licks my fingers.

* * *

In the car on the way home, I reach for my mobile phone. Rita is staring blankly at the car dashboard. 'What the hell do I tell everyone? I can't face making the same awful phone call six times over.'

Rita snaps out of her trance. 'You ring Des and I'll ring Duke. We can ask them to pass on the news to the others.'

I nod. 'I say we just give them a version of the truth for the time being.'

'How do you mean?' says Rita.

'I mean we tell Des and Duke that Star has been withdrawn from the race due to injury. And that we'll have more information for them later.'

Rita looks at me sympathetically. 'Okay.'

After ringing Des, Rita calls Duke. I grip the steering wheel tightly, thoughts churning over and over in my mind. 'This is all my fault.'

Rita turns and looks at me. 'What do you mean?'

'Me, buying a racehorse. Like I was picking one off the screen at the bookies to bet on. I never once stopped to consider that Star is just flesh and blood.' Rita turns her head away and stares out of the window. 'I've been too busy playing the big "I Am" in front of my mates.'

'Andy, I think you're -'

I cut her short. 'I mean, who did I think I was. Barney bloody Curley?'

As we approach the outskirts of Nottingham, it starts raining again. My driving becomes erratic. 'Eight months on, what has my brilliant "Colwick Park Coup" plan actually amounted to?' Tears for Star trickle down my face, mixed with tears of self-pity.

'Persecuting yourself won't help – and please, keep your eyes on the road, will you?'

'Fuck all, that's what! All I've managed to do is ruin the life of a beautiful filly and succeed in looking like a prize twat in front of everyone!' The car's traction intermittently loses grip and begins to slide on the road's slippery surface. Through the zig-zag of the windscreen wipers, a car approaches at speed. I see it late.

'Annddyyyy!'

I swerve the car and head off the road into a ditch. Slamming the brakes on, I narrowly miss a tree. My head starts spinning. Everything goes quiet.

'Bloody hell! You could have killed us!'

I throw myself forward onto the steering wheel. 'Fuck! I'm sorry!'

Rita caresses my arm. '*I'm* sorry, too. I shouldn't have shouted. I was just …'

'It's okay,' I mumble. I remain slumped against the wheel. I start to cry.

'It's alright,' says Rita, rubbing my shoulder. 'It's been a stressful day.'

'And it's barely afternoon!'

Rita places her hand on my arm and gently turns my head towards her. 'How about I drive the last bit?'

'Okay.' I unlock my seatbelt and get out of the driver's seat. Outside, the rain has stopped. I trudge around the back of the car, and without another word, we swap places.

* * *

Twenty minutes later I unlock the front door to the flat. I check the time on the living room wall. Two thirty. My heart sinks. In precisely one hour, the six-furlong sprint at Colwick Park will go off without Star. I turn and look at Rita. She looks drained.

'C'mon,' she says. 'Let's go to bed. I don't know about you, but I'm done with today.'

I manage a faint smile and nod. Walking to the living room windows I draw the curtains, then take the telephone off the hook. In the bedroom, Rita undresses in silence in the half darkness. She glances at me, stood in the entrance to the bedroom.

'C'mon,' she says.

Hanging on the door frame at right-angles are our new race day outfits, complete with our shiny owner badges. I brush past them and in doing so, they fall to the floor. I leave them lying there in a heap.

18

★ ANDY ★

In the days that follow Star's operation, I throw myself into my postal round. Early afternoon, Friday, I find myself alone in the flat. I sit down on the sofa and drink a can of beer, eyeing the telephone on the living room table. I drink it quickly and fetch another one. Returning to the sofa I crack it open, take a long swig, stare at the telephone again and light a cigarette. I breath in deeply and slowly exhale. I pick up the telephone receiver and punch in Ray's number, just as I hear the key turn in the front door. I replace the handset.

Rita appears in the doorway to the living room. 'Hi.'

'Hi.' I remain on the sofa. 'How did it go with the midwife?'

She removes her coat and enters the room. 'Fine. She's really nice. Her name is Bernadette. She made me feel as though the safe delivery of our baby is her number one priority in life.'

'That's great,' I say.

Rita looks disapprovingly at my cigarette. 'Not in here, Andy,' she says, pointing with her eyes to her tummy.

'Err, no. Sorry.' I stub out my cigarette and take the ashtray to the kitchen. When I re-join her, she's lying spread-eagled on the sofa. Beside her, a wad of antenatal information leaflets lay scattered on the living room table.

'My new health regime starts today,' she says.

'No glass of wine for you tonight, then?' This doesn't come out as intended. I fumble my half-empty can of beer self-consciously.

'No. As of today, I'm packing in the booze. But you can fetch me a diet coke from the fridge, if you like?'

'Sure.' In the kitchen, I pour a can of coke from the fridge into a glass and add some ice. I leave it beside her on the living room table.

'Thanks.' A short silence falls over us. It's Rita who breaks it. 'I've asked Bernadette to set up an appointment for our first ultra-sound.'

'Bloody hell.'

Rita looks at me. 'What does that mean?'

'Bloody hell, as in, that's exciting. What did you think I meant?' I look at her.

She's biting her nails. 'That's when they'll be able to check to see if the embryo is okay.'

I take a long swig of beer.

'You will be there, won't you?' she says.

'Of course I will.' I meet her glance. She looks nervous. It isn't like her.

'Promise?'

'Of course. I promise. This is my baby too.'

'I know,' she says, biting her nails again. Another short silence falls over the room. Rita changes the subject. 'So, how was your day?'

'Oh, you know …' I reply, staring at my beer can as though I was addressing it rather than her. 'The usual.'

'Have you rung Ray yet?'

'I was just about to when you came home.'

More silence. 'I wonder how she is?' I nod silently. 'Don't you wonder too?' she says.

'I think of little else - her and our baby.'

Rita frowns. 'What is it, Andy?'

I take a swig of beer. 'Of course I want to know how Star is. It's just that, I'm …'

'What?'

'Scared. Scared of finding out. I mean, I guess this means the end of her racing career? And yet I'm deliberately putting off finding out because …'

'What?'

'Because … oh, never mind.' I spring out of my chair and cross the living room. 'I think I'll head out for a bit.'

Rita looks at me, trying to read me. I notice her glance at the leaflets she brought home with her. 'I just thought we could … where are you going?'

'I don't know. Just out for a walk.'

I stand in the entrance to the hallway, trapped in her gaze. She looks more sad than angry.

'See you later,' I mumble and head towards the front door.

* * *

I close it self-consciously behind me. Before long, I'm wandering aimlessly along Sneinton Boulevard. The atmosphere in the air is close, humid. I stop and look up at the sky. A storm is brewing. Before I know it, I find myself walking in the direction of the cemetery - my sanctuary, the only place in Sneinton I'm able to think clearly these days. I veer off the stony pathway and walk across the grass to mum and dad's graves. For a while I just stand there in silent contemplation. Fatherhood. I think about what the word means to me. It sounds daunting. I stand before mum and dad's graves like a vulnerable child and with that comes some clarity of thought. If ever there was a time I needed them around, it is now.

19

★ DES ★

I'm sat in my armchair reading the racing page in the Nottingham Evening Post. I put it down, pick up the telephone and dial Andy's number. It rings and rings. No answer. I stand up and gaze absent-mindedly out of the front room window. Eventually I return to my armchair and my newspaper. A couple of moments later the telephone rings. I pick up.

'Andy – what's going on?'

'Grandpa?'

I smile. 'Kyle. How are you?'

Kyle mumbles something inaudible, followed by a question. 'Did Star win?'

I sigh. 'She didn't actually run, Kyle. Andy rang on the morning of the race. She's picked up some kind of injury.'

Kyle goes silent. Eventually, he says, 'it's nothing serious, is it?'

'I don't know. I'm waiting on more information. That's why I delayed ringing you, you see? I promise to let you know when I find out more.' The line remains silent. 'So, how's life?' I say. The silence continues. 'Kyle. Are you still there?'

'Not so great.'

'How do you mean?'

'I got into some trouble,' says Kyle.

'What kind of trouble?'

'A fight. At school. With Phil, a boy in my class.'

'I see. What did you fight about?' I wedge the phone between my shoulder and my chin and begin rolling a cigarette.

'He was calling me names. I couldn't tell if he was like, joking or not. I find it difficult, reading people.' He goes quiet again. 'On and on he went. In the end I decided he wasn't joking, so I lashed out.'

'How do you mean, "lashed out"?' More silence from the other end of the phone line. 'Kyle?'

'I … I punched him. Got sent to the head.'

I light my roll- up. 'What was he joking about, Kyle?'

'Oh, you know …'

'No, I don't know. That's why I'm asking you,' I say impatiently. I re-track. 'Sorry. What was he making jokes about?'

'The colour of my skin,' Kyle mumbles.

'Weren't there any teachers about?'

'Yeah. Mr Wood.'

'The careers advisor?'

'Yeah - but he wasn't close enough to hear what Phil was calling me.'

'A person's colour isn't the kind of thing one makes jokes about, Kyle, full-stop.' I think for a moment. 'Though punching him wasn't the best way to resolve things.' More silence from the other end of the line. 'Anyway, I hope this Phil got sent to the head as well? I mean, he provoked you.'

'Yeah. He did.'

I take a long draw on my roll-up. 'Can I give you some advice? To help you avoid this sort of thing happening again?'

'Okay.'

'This Phil, he's what you call ignorant.'

'What does ignorant mean?'

'Someone who is ignorant lacks knowledge or awareness. Phil is ignorant because he thinks less of you because of the colour of your skin.' Kyle mumbles something by way of agreement. 'The next time you find yourself in a situation like that, try to rise above it.'

'How do you mean?'

'Rise above their ignorance. Show the person who is hassling you that you are better than them. Use their ignorance to your advantage.'

'I don't follow. Give me an example.'

'Okay.' I think for a moment before continuing. 'A long time ago, around a year before I left Barbados, a group of white Barbadians thought less of me because of the colour of my skin. I had a job that they didn't think I could do as well as them.'

'Why not?'

I shrug my shoulders. 'Ignorance, I guess. But do you know what?'

'No.'

'I showed them – proved to all of them that I was at least as good as any of those white fellas, if not better. And all without raising a fist.'

'I'll try and remember that next time, Grandpa.'

I smile and change the subject. 'It's not long until you sit your GCSEs, is it?'

'No. Just a couple of weeks to go.'

'Then will you make me a promise?' I say.

Silence. 'That depends what it is.'

I smile. 'That until then, you focus all of your energy on doing the best you can in your exams? Will you do that for me?' More silence. 'Kyle?'

'Yeah. I promise.'

'Good lad. And in the meantime, be good to your mum, okay?'

'Okay,' Kyle says.

'In fact, is she there? I'd like a quick word.'

'She's not back from work yet.'

'Okay. Well send her my love, will you?'

'I will.'

'Good - and as soon as I hear anything about Star, you'll be the first to know.'

'Okay. And Grandpa?'

'Yes?'

The line goes silent for a few seconds. 'Thanks.'

20

★ ANDY ★

R*at-a-tat-tat.* I wake from a booze induced snooze, startled and disorientated. *Rat-a-tat-tat.*

A voice travels down the hallway.

'Hello? Anyone home?'

Fuck. It's Des. Flashback to April last year. Dad, calling to me through the letterbox. *Please let me in, son?* Dad. Begging me to open the door so he could apologise, ease his conscience for the way he'd treated me after mum died. I hear a second voice. I creep along the hallway and press my ear against the door.

'He *should* be home, Des.' Rita too. I watch the front door handle turn. I take two paces back and in walks Rita with Des in tow.

He looks at me with a surprised expression. 'Andy? I didn't think you were …'

'Hello Des, Hi Rita.' I'm unsure what to say or do next.

Rita has had enough. 'For God's sake, Andy! Invite Des in, offer him a drink and just tell him what's going on, will you?'

* * *

I fetch two beers from the fridge. I ask Des to sit down opposite me in the living room. Rita leaves us to it - and heads into the bedroom, where she sets about clearing a space to make room for a cot.

Des looks up from his beer and fixes me with his gaze. 'Why the long silence? It isn't like you.'

I twitch nervously. 'I'm sorry. I just haven't been able to face up to telling you what's been going on. You of all people.'

'Tell me what?'

'That … Star's run her last race.' I glimpse at Des. He's making a brave go of hiding the shock he must be feeling. I take a swig of beer and fill him in on the events of *that* morning. The call from Ray, Rita and I charging up to the stables and the ultimatum Ray's vet gave me about Star's eye. 'Giving him permission to remove it, Des, it was …' My words tail off. 'The vet needed an answer there and then. If I hadn't said yes, he said there was a good chance that the infection would spread and become life threatening.' Des looks at me solemnly. 'The worse thing was, that by telling him to do it …' My words tail off again.

'Would mean the end of her career.' Des completes my sentence for me.

'Yes – and the end of our dream.'

Des takes a mouthful of beer and stares out of the window. I remain silent. Out of the corner of my eye, I see Rita hovering in the bedroom doorway. She sends me a compassionate smile. I wave her over. She joins me and sits on the edge of the sofa. She rests her hand on my knee. Des gets up and sits beside me on the other side. He looks me in the eye. 'Have you spoken to Ray lately?' he says.

'Not since the day she was operated on. I was going to, but lost my bottle. He must think I've left the country.' Rita goes into the kitchen and returns with two fresh beers and a cola. 'But I've given Star's situation a lot of thought these past few days. Rita, I want you to hear this too.'

'Okay,' she says.

I pour my beer into my glass and take a swig. 'I'm going to ring Ray tomorrow, arrange a meeting. I'll ask him about places who take in former racehorses - livery yards, that kind of thing. Somewhere Star can be cared for in the manner she deserves.' I look at Des and Rita in turn. 'What do you think?'

Rita puts her arms around me. 'I think it's for the best, considering what's happened. What do you think, Des?'

Des smiles at me through his sadness. 'I agree. We have a duty of care to her.'

I look him in the eye. 'I know how attached you've become to her since day one – and more recently, how attached Kyle has become to her too. That's why it's important that I find somewhere where we will be able to visit her - somewhere we can drop by whenever we want, help with her feed, muck her out, whatever – or just watch her grazing with the other horses. Somewhere not too far out of Nottingham.'

Des nods. 'Just don't delay telling the others. I know how difficult this must have been for you, telling me – but you'll feel better still once everyone knows.'

'Yeah,' I say, twitching my fingers. 'Of course.'

Des senses my underlying anxiety. 'What is it, Andy?'

I'm desperate for a smoke. I fiddle with the cigarette carton in my hand instead. 'I just feel so bad about it. Like I've strung you all along, sold everyone a dream which I'm no longer able to deliver. I just wanted to give everyone the chance of making some money, down the road at our local course. It's amounted to absolutely nothing. Telling everyone is going to be so hard. Looking them in the eye, admitting failure.'

'Now you're talking nonsense,' says Des. 'Is it your fault Star's eye got infected?'

Rita rubs my shoulder. 'Des is right.'

'And above all, you're doing right by Star at the time it counts the most,' adds Des. A short silence falls over the room.

'I'll ring Ray tomorrow and arrange to see him. As soon as that's set up, I'll tell the others.'

Des pats my knee, drains his beer and raises himself. 'It's time I made tracks.' Rita and I follow him to the door. Des opens it, but before leaving he turns and faces me. 'Don't ever forget, Andy.'

'Forget what?'

'Just how close you were.'

'How do you mean?' I say.

To pulling it off.' And with that, he's gone.

21

★ ANDY ★

Early the next morning, I phone Ray.

'Hello Andy.' His broad Nottinghamshire brogue crackles down the line.

'Sorry I've left things so long.'

'It's understandable, given what's happened.'

'It's been difficult. Facing up to it.'

'I get that. No problem.'

I open the kitchen window and light a cigarette. 'How is she?'

'Well, she's over her op. You must come up and see her.'

'That's why I'm ringing.'

I avoid any small-talk – and our conversation lasts just long enough for us to agree a meeting on Friday, the day after tomorrow.

* * *

I punch in Duke's number, but five digits in, lose my nerve. I replace the handset. *I can't face telling him. I can't face telling any of them.* Instead, I stall again - opening each call with a grovelling apology for leaving things so long; throwing in a lie in a pathetic attempt to curry favour about how I've been ill. I end each call by promising to explain everything at the King Billy, the day after tomorrow in person. The last person I ring is Des.

'I'm meeting Ray at the stable on Friday morning – and have asked everyone to be at the King Billy that evening at eight.'

'How did they take the news?' says Des. The line goes silent. 'You did tell them, didn't you?'

'I …'

'Andy.'

'Des, it's …'

'Never mind. I'm not interested in making you feel worse than you do.'

'I just think that after seeing Star again with my own eyes – and after telling Ray what I intend to do, well – it will prepare me better for sharing the news, that's all.'

'Each to their own.'

'Thanks. For trying to understand.'

'Just one thing,' he says.

'What's that?'

'I must let Kyle know what's happened. He's been worried.'

'Sure. Of course.'

* * *

That afternoon, Rita and I take the bus in to town, where we buy our first ever mobile phones – two identical black Motorola ones, with bright green LCD panels. I also buy my first home answerphone machine. We spend the rest of the afternoon looking at cots. Reaching a decision over Star's future, devastating as it is, has at least brought some respite. I feel less distracted, more in tune with Rita – and I make a mental note of the traditional wooden cot she so clearly has her heart set on. Rita's bump is beginning to show.

'Pregnancy suits you,' I say, nuzzling her neck.

She laughs, turns to me and we kiss.

* * *

The following afternoon after I clock off from work, Rita greets me at the door.

'Guess what?' she says.

'What?'

'I've had a letter from the hospital with the date of our ultra-sound appointment!'

'Great,' I say, taking off my jacket in the hallway. 'When is it?'

'This Friday, Nottingham General at three thirty.'

'That's the same day I'm seeing Ray. Don't worry though, it won't take long.'

Rita looks anxious. 'Can't you rearrange it?' she says.

'It will be fine. Don't worry. I'll make sure I'm at the hospital in plenty of time.'

22

★ ANDY ★

At five to eleven on a humid July morning, I pull into Nine Elms Stables. I've rehearsed word for word what I'm going to say to Ray on the drive in. We shake hands in the entrance to the grey stoned cottage, before he leads me into his office. We sit down opposite one another at his large, messy desk.

'Good to see you, Andy. Coffee?'

'No thanks, I'm fine.'

I look down at my hands in my lap. Then I look up and meet his gaze.

'Ray, I've decided to take Star out of training.'

'I see.'

'Although things haven't turned out the way we'd planned, I want to thank you for all of your hard work. I know that you had Star in peak condition ahead of what should have been our big day …' My words tail off. I quickly gather myself. 'Anyway, let me know of any outstanding monies I owe, send me an invoice and I'll get it paid up immediately.'

Ray looks at me philosophically. 'What happened was tragic Andy, but –'

I cut him short. 'It is – but all that matters now, is Star's future well-being. So, any advice you might have about how we find a suitable home for her – a stable for retired thoroughbreds, that kind of thing - then I'd be really grateful.'

'Of course - there are several places I can recommend. And I'm delighted that unlike some owners I've trained for, you're putting Star's wellbeing first.' Ray smiles at me and I return the gesture. 'But before rushing into anything, there's something I want you to see.'

* * *

Turning right behind the cottage, Ray leads me through a thicket of elm trees to a part of the stable grounds I've not previously visited. Before long, we arrive at the edge of an oval shaped all-weather gallop.

'Right. Up here,' he says. I follow him up a rickety flight of steps to a raised wooden platform, not unlike the structure overlooking the six-furlong turf gallop. Ray turns and faces me. Handing me a spare pair of binoculars he says, 'Now, watch. I think you're going to enjoy this.'

Raising his binoculars to his eyes, Ray focuses on the bend at the far end of the track. I do the same. All is still and silent – until a chestnut colour racehorse wearing some elaborate yellow headgear suddenly appears, galloping around the top turn. Hugging the inner rail, he takes the corner at speed and straightens up for home, cajoled all the way by his work rider. They leave a blaze of fibresand trailing in their wake. The horse's pilot, wearing reflective goggles and a green scarf covering his mouth, slaps the horse down his near side as they pass the finishing line beneath us. It was an impressive display, but one that leaves me confused, not to mention a little wary.

'Are you trying to interest me in another horse?' I say.

'What?'

'If you think I'm ready to buy a replacement for Star, then you've got me all wrong!' I make to pass him.

Ray stops me. 'Easy Andy.'

'Then have a heart, will you?' I say. 'What do you take me for?'

'Listen,' he laughs, nervously. 'There's been a misunderstanding.' Ray looks downwards towards the foot of the tower and points at the horse and rider below. 'Look at them, Andy,' he says. *'Closely.'*

I do as he says and watch the work rider dismount. He unravels his green scarf and raises his goggles off his face. Or *her* face, I should say. It's Ellie. Turning her attention to the horse, she unstraps the yellow headgear to reveal a second familiar face, despite the unfamiliar eye-patch. Star.

23

★ ANDY ★

Ellie calls up to me. 'I thought the green scarf might have given me away?' I gawp at her, completely dumbfounded. 'Obviously not, going by the look on yer face!' She smiles broadly and pats Star down the neck. 'But I do get you, not recognising this girl,' she says. 'It's like a miracle, isn't it?'

I turn to Ray. A thousand questions ping around inside my head like a ball in a pinball machine. Eventually one comes to the surface. 'How did you even get her near the gallops, let alone running like that with just one eye? I mean, she hates oval tracks, doesn't she?'

Ray puts his arm around my shoulder. 'Sorry if I startled you, Andy. Ellie and I just wanted it to be a surprise.'

My jaw drops. 'A surprise? That has to be the understatement of the century!'

Ray smiles. 'You're right. Star used to hate oval tracks - when she had sight in both of her eyes. But since her op and following a lot of patient rehab, she now loves them - so long as they are left-turning ones.'

'So, I'm not dreaming all of this then?'

Ray smiles at me. 'No Andy, you're not dreaming – though perhaps, like Ellie says, it is a bit of a miracle?'

I nod. 'You're not wrong there.'

Ray turns to face me. 'Now,' he says, with just a hint of playful smugness, 'what was that you were saying earlier about taking Star out of training?'

The smile returns to my face. 'Very funny.'

'Let's head back to the cottage – and I'll explain everything that's been happening with Star since you were here last.'

* * *

Ray hands me a mug of coffee. Removing his whiskey from the bottom drawer of his desk, he says, 'fancy a splash?'

'Yes please. You'd better make it a double.'

Ray smiles and adds a generous measure. Passing me the mug, he says, 'so where should I start?'

'How about from the moment Rita and I left here, completely heartbroken?'

Ray takes a mouthful of his drink. 'Okay. So later that afternoon, while Star was recuperating, I drove into Edwinstowe to run some errands. On my way I switched on the car radio. Quite by chance, I came upon a programme about the life of Ray Charles.'

'The blind R&B singer?'

'Yeah, the very same. Do you know any of his stuff?'

Quite what the life and times of Ray Charles could possibly have to do with Star's transformation is beyond me, but I go with the flow.

'Sure,' I say. '"Hit The Road, Jack", "What I Say, Parts I and II", "I Gotta woman."'

Ray looks surprised. 'I'm impressed.'

'Mum and dad had a Greatest Hits album. They played it a lot when I was growing up.'

Ray nods. 'One of the things I learnt from this radio programme was that Ray Charles wasn't born blind. Did you know that?'

'No, I can't say that I did.'

Ray continues. 'It happened when he was seven years old. In an attempt to try to save the sight in his good eye, doctors removed his right one. Ultimately, they failed and before long, he lost his eyesight all together.'

'That's awful.'

Ray nods. 'After I got back to the stables, I made myself some dinner. I ate it in front of the telly with a glass of red wine and soon forgot all about the radio programme. But later my thoughts returned to it, which is when something struck me - the quality I most admired about him, Ray Charles that is.' He leans forward and offers me another splash of whiskey in my coffee. I accept.

'And what was that?'

'That he didn't let his disability stop him from becoming the best R & B artist of his generation. Which is when something else occurred to me.'

'Go on,' I say.

'That some people, when losing one of their senses, excel with another. They compensate. In other words, they turn their disability into a strength. And do you know what?'

'What?' I'm intrigued.

'Animals are just the same.' A short silence falls over the room. 'That evening, as I worked my way through my bottle of claret, I remembered a horse that ran on the flat in the seventies who only had one eye. His name was Belper. John Dunlop trained him. Belper lost his sight in his right eye, just like Star. Before ringing Belper's owners to break the tragic news, an idea came to him. It's funny, because his thinking reminded me of something Des' grandson said, the first time he came up here.'

'Who, Kyle?'

'Yeah, Kyle – about horses having 350-degree vision. Bright spark, that lad.' Ray pauses and takes a sip of his drink. 'Aware that Belper retained 175-degree vision, albeit exclusively out of his left eye, Dunlop decided to try racing Belper on his left-turning oval gallop, with a patch over his right eye socket.'

'Blimey. How did it go?' I say.

'Well, with the inner rail helping to guide Belper, Dunlop discovered something remarkable. Not only did he cope really well with the tight, left-handed turns, he was soon running better than he ever had!'

'You're having me on?' I say.

'I'm not. Wait, there's more. Not only did Belper make a successful return to racing, he went on to win six races at Brighton!'

'Get away!' I almost choke on my coffee.

'Straight up,' says Ray. 'The radio programme about Ray Charles and John Dunlop's experiment with Belper, well – they led me to think, why not try something similar with Star? I figured we had nothing to lose. And as you saw earlier with your own eyes, it's paid off.'

* * *

Ellie appears in the doorway. Ray looks at her. 'Ellie, join us' he say, 'and explain to Andy how we nurtured Star back into training. After all, it was you who did all the hard graft.'

Ellie pulls up a stool, while Ray pours her a coffee. With

a twinkle in her eyes, she looks at me and says, 'have you recovered from the shock yet?'

'Let's say I'm still in the process of recovery,' I laugh.

Ellie smiles and takes a sip of her coffee. 'So, a couple of days after Star's eye healed over, I was out organising first lot. As I passed her box, she started kicking at her door, as though to say, "don't forget about me!" I mentioned this to Ray. We agreed it was a good sign; that she was feeling good in herself again. That was the day Ray first mentioned Belper to me – and asked my opinion on whether we could try something similar with Star?'

Ray interjects. 'Now, I'm not privy as to exactly how John Dunlop nurtured Belper back to the gallops. But I've been around racehorses long enough to have a few ideas of my own.'

Ellie continues. 'Before taking Star anywhere near the gallops, Ray came up with a plan.'

'What was that?' I say.

Ellie takes a swig of coffee. 'That before we even tried cantering her, that we worked on building up her confidence on her blind right side.'

'Do you recall my vet talking about the psychological issues Star could face?' says Ray.

I nod. 'Well, I thought about what he said and what I concluded was this: that minimising the sense of fear Star would experience by sighting things late on her blind side would be crucial, if we were ever to stand a chance of getting her onto the gallops again.'

'So, what did you do?' I say. Ellie smiles. 'What is it?'

'No, it's nothing. It's just going to sound funny, that's all, describing the process to you now,' she says, adding, 'though, believe me when I say, it was really nerve-racking at first.'

Ellie drinks the last of her coffee, before continuing. 'Behind the stabling area we have a large, airy barn. It's illuminated by a lot of natural light. Every morning and afternoon, I would take Star there for a couple of hours at a time. Allowing plenty of spare lead, I would tie Star to a post in the centre of the barn. It was a precautionary step, in case she suddenly panicked and reared up. This wasn't text book stuff, after all – neither Ray nor I had any idea how she was going to react to the exercises. Anyway, after making sure that she was completely relaxed, I would move out of her line of vision. Then, very slowly, I would approach her along her blind right side from behind. Upon sighting me the first time, she reared up on her hind legs - kicked and whined. It completely spooked her. I was lucky not to get kicked over. But once I'd calmed her down - after she realised it was just me - I repeated the exercise, rewarding her with carrots or polo mints each time. Slowly but surely, through sheer repetition, she began reacting less and less when I appeared in her line of vision.'

'Horses are intelligent creatures. If you build up a level of trust with them, like Ellie with Star, they'll walk through fire for you,' says Ray.

Ellie continues. 'A day or two later, Ray and I decided it was time to try her out on the left-turning all-weather gallops.'

'The first time we took her up there, I told Ellie to give her no more than a gentle work out,' Ray says. 'I looked on cautiously as Ellie walked her out onto the track. It was interesting, Andy. Do you know what Star did as soon Ellie got her into a canter?' I give Ray a blank look and shrug my shoulders. 'Cantered towards the inside rail. It gave her good left eye something to focus on. She followed its curve and began moving with ease,' says Ellie. 'Over the days that followed, she was happy in me gradually increasing our speed – peaking with the gallop you saw this morning.'

A short silence falls over the three of us. Ray is the first to speak. 'Can I be one hundred percent honest with you, Andy?'

'Of course.'

'Okay. Well, from what I have seen of her these past couple of days, Star is a faster horse racing left-handed with just one-eye than she ever would have been racing over a straight six-furlongs with full eyesight.'

'Really?'

'Oh yeah,' he says. 'It isn't that she wasn't any good before. She was. All I am saying is that she is even faster now.'

Ellie backs him up. 'Star has compensated. And from what I've seen of her, I believe that she's only going to continue to improve.'

'So, in other words, you could say she's done a complete "Ray Charles!"'

Ray and Ellie join in my laughter. 'Yes,' Ray says. 'That she has!'

* * *

Ellie leaves to oversee second lot. Ray and I sit in momentary silence, finishing our coffees. 'Before I forget,' he says eventually, 'I've been in touch with the racing authorities. There are changes that need to be made to Star's passport.'

'She has a passport?'

'Yeah, all racehorses do.'

'Good,' I say. 'Keep it locked in that bottom draw with the whiskey, Ray - we don't want her doing a runner now!'

Ray joins in my laughter. 'Seriously, she won't be

allowed to race until her passport has been amended, stating that in future she will be racing with only fifty percent vision.'

'I see.' Something suddenly strikes me – and I can't hide a look of disappointment sweeping across my face. Ray picks up on it. 'Something wrong?'

'More of a delayed realisation I guess.'

'What's that?'

'It's just that given Star's new liking for racing left-handed, I guess Colwick Park is no longer the place for us to try and land our coup?'

'I'm afraid that's true, Andy. I mean, I'm not saying that she isn't up to winning a race there in future - rather than, right now, an oval left-handed track would play more to her strengths.'

'No. I get it.'

Ray continues. 'The good news is that I'm confident she will run well at any left-handed oval course in the country. Take your pick, there's loads of them: Chester, Epsom, Belper's Brighton of course, or closer to home, Southwell or Wolverhampton - any of these courses will be right up her alley now. But wherever we end up running her, there is one thing we do need to be wary of.'

'And what's that?'

'The draw. This is where we'll require a bit of luck. Given her eye condition, the plum draw for Star will always be stall one, bang against the rail. Stall two or three will probably be okay too, thus giving us a little leeway.'

'And race tactics?' I say.

'Her best chance of winning will be to break quickly out of the gate and attempt to make all. By grabbing the rail and running her race from the front, we'll reduce the chances of her getting spooked by challengers on her blind right-side.'

'Smart thinking,' I say.

'The fitting of blinkers will help. Running her this way, the plan is that none of her rivals will be quick enough to mount a challenge!'

'I can't wait to see her run,' I say.

'After factoring in her low handicap mark, she should have so much in hand, it's possible she won't see another horse until she passes the unsaddling enclosure!' Ray catches the glint in my eye. He goes on. 'Wherever we decide to run, in the build up to her race, I'll have Ellie schooling Star to jump out of the gate like a scalded cat – and whoever rides her on the day, I will personally ensure that our racing instructions are followed to the letter.'

'You've really thought this through, Ray.'

'Ellie and I. Yes, we have.'

A short silence falls over us. 'Thanks, Ray.'

'What for?'

'For not giving up on her.'

'Don't thank me.' Ray points heavenwards. 'Thank Ray Charles!'

I nod, laughing, before yawning spontaneously.

Ray laughs. 'You've had a lot to take in. I think we're all done for today, unless there's anything else you want to ask?'

'No. Though I would love to see her, before I go.'

* * *

We approach Star's box. Ray whistles a shrill sound on our way over and all of a sudden there she is, peaking her head out.

Ray says, 'look who's come visit, girl?'

Star is wearing an eye-patch. She turns her head to her side and ogles me with her left eye.

I slip a carrot out of my pocket and offer it up to her. She takes it while I ruffle her mane. After she's eaten, she licks my fingers in recognition. I turn and face Ray. 'Will you do me a favour?'

'Of course,' he says.

'Remove her eye-patch. I want to see her as she really is.'

'Are you sure?'

'Yeah.' Ray leans forward and carefully removes the black cotton patch. 'Does she feel any pain where her eye once was?'

'No, the skin has completely healed over. Just as though an eye ball was never there.'

I tilt my head in towards her. She mirrors my movement. As she turns her head back into profile, I look into her beautiful deep brown eye and for a moment, catch my reflection. Very slowly I move my hand across her face, onto her blind side – and without the slightest twitch, she lets me run my fingers very gently across the rough layer of skin that has grown over her eye socket. Then I take her head in both of my hands and plant a kiss on the centre of her striking white blaze.

24

★ ANDY ★

I pull out of Nine Elms Stables and roll down my driver seat window. It's turned into a beautiful afternoon. Keeping my eyes on the road, I turn on the car radio and swivel the dial in search of a music station. I settle on a retro soul one and before long, I'm keeping the beat, funky drummer style, slapping the steering wheel along with James Brown and The JBs. After that, I accompany Al Green on one of his old hits before the song fades out into the commercial break. Continuing on through the Nottinghamshire countryside, the music returns - and I call out in recognition of the funky intro to 'Shining Star', by Earth, Wind and Fire. I crank up the volume and smile as the lyrics take on a new meaning.

'When you wish upon a star,
Your dreams will take you very far, yeah
But when you wish upon a dream
Life ain't always what it seems, oh yeah ...'

My mobile phone vibrates in my jeans pocket. I turn the radio down and wriggle the phone free. 'Andy speaking.'

'Where the fuck have you been?'

'Oh fuck … what time is it? Rita, I'm *so* sorry …'

'You promised me you'd be there …'

'I don't know what to –'

'I'm on my way home from the ultra-sound appointment. On my own, as though our baby has no dad. The way those nurses looked at me, the sickening pity in their eyes. It ruined everything.'

'I'm so sorry.'

'You're not! Otherwise, you'd have *been* there!'

The line goes silent. 'Rita, let me –'

'No Andy - you listen to me! I've been there for you during this difficult time with Star - supported you, stood by you. That's because as well as caring about Star, above all, I care about *you.* I've realised lately what she really means to you. But today – the very first time I ask you to be there for me, you're nowhere to be seen. It leaves me doubting your desire to really be a dad because, do you know what? I'm not feeling it …'

I hear Rita's tears down the line and want the ground to swallow me up.

'But I am ready to …'

'Then you should have been there today!' she shouts. The line goes quiet. The silence seems to last for ages, though in reality it's probably only a few seconds. It's Rita who breaks it. 'In case you're interested, my embryo looks healthy. We have a due date of October the fourteenth … in case you're still around then.' I make to say something but Rita cuts me short again. 'Don't get in touch unless you're serious about being a part of our baby's life!'

She hangs up and the line goes dead.

'Fuck!' I thump the steering wheel. 'Fuck, Fuck, Fuck!'

* * *

Back at the flat, I fetch a can of lager. I drink it in the living room. I totally get why Rita is pissed off, but resent not getting the chance to explain to her the reason I got held up.

I dial her mobile. It cuts straight to voicemail. I ring her home number but there's no reply. I light a cigarette and smoke it out of the kitchen window. I check the time. I'm due at the King Billy in less than an hour. I stub out my cigarette, lie down on the sofa and close my eyes. I toss and turn, unable to rest up. My mind is in overdrive, churning over the events of the day. I give up my power nap and try to get my head straight instead. Falling out with Rita isn't great preparation for sharing tonight's exciting news with everyone, so I compartmentalise it – 'park it' – in the hope that Rita and I can resolve our problems in the days to come. I try to visualize everyone's faces when I break the news to them about Star and my mood lifts. I stand up, brush myself down, grab my denim jacket and head to the pub.

* * *

It's a balmy July evening. After stopping by the cashpoint on the corner of Manvers Road, I enter the saloon bar ~~at~~ bang on eight. Pat the landlord greets me.

'All right, Youth?'

'Not bad, Pat – and you? Pint of Stones please.'

'Right you are, son.'

As Pat pours my pint I reach into my pocket. 'Stick this behind the bar, will you?'

I hand him a fifty-pound note. Pat nods and takes the

money. I take a sip from my pint and look around. At the far corner table, I see them, instantly recognisable by Des' pork pie hat. On my way over, I pass the wall mounted juke-box. I stop and scan through the sixties-soul list and smile. I slip a coin into the slot and make my selection.

* * *

Arriving at the table, seven anxious faces meet my gaze.

'Evening everyone,' I say. Seven mumbled replies come back at me.

'Here,' says Des, pulling out an empty chair beside him.

'Thanks, Des - but I'll remain standing for now.' You could hear a pin drop. I reach for my cigarettes and the sound of my lighter breaks the silence.

'So, what's going on?' says One-Armed. It's clear from the sound of his voice, that the pint sat in front of him, isn't the first one he's had.

'Yeah. What's happening with Star?' says Big Les.

I clear my throat. To my left, Des appears fidgety and nervous. The song I selected on the jukebox, *'What I Say, Parts One and Two'* by Ray Charles, begins. The music appears to relax him a little. He looks up at me.

'Brother Ray. Nice choice!'

'For the love of God,' says One-Armed. 'Can we just let Andy speak?'

'Sorry,' says Des, sheepishly. I place my hand on his shoulder. 'If you think you love Ray Charles *now* Des, you're going to love him even more by the time I've finished.' He gives me an uncertain smile as I press on. 'Alright. So, two days ago, when I rang you all about meeting me here tonight, it was to share some really heavy news. You see, on the morning of Star's race, Ray discovered that her right eye was swollen and inflamed.'

'Bloody hell. How is it now?' says Glen.

One-Armed clumsily raises himself from his stool. Glaring at Glen, he says, 'If people stop interrupting, maybe he'll get the chance to tell us!'

'Easy,' says Sammy, easing One-Armed back to a seated position.

As The Ray Charles song finishes, I resume. 'Her eye was oozing puss. Ray's vet told me that the infection was life threatening, unless it was removed. I had no choice but to give him my permission to take it out.' I stub out my cigarette and take a mouthful of beer. Everyone is hanging on my next word. 'I returned to Nottingham that afternoon, certain Star's career was over. Every minute of every day since, I've spent wondering how I could break this news to all of you – that Star would never race again; that our dream is over. Much as I tried, I couldn't bring myself to do it. I couldn't bring myself to talk to Ray, either. Then two days ago, I faced facts. I rang Ray and arranged a meeting. This took place earlier today, up at the stables. I went up there for the purpose of taking Star out of training, to arrange to have her transferred to a home for injured thoroughbreds.' I take a mouthful of beer and light myself another cigarette. 'But when I got up there, it quickly became clear to me that something, well, miraculous had happened.' I then tell them how Ray had shown me a horse burning up the gallops unaware that it was Star; how his analogy about Ray Charles triggered his memory of the one-eyed Belper – and how Belper's story inspired Ray and Ellie to try to coax Star back into training, transforming her in the process into a one-eyed left-turning oval course specialist. By the time I'm finished, everyone is gawping at me in wide-eyed disbelief. 'So, fellas, it's like this. Not only is Star better than ever,' I conclude, 'she's ready to race!!' I watch my friends faces as they process my words.

'Well, that's a relief,' says One-Armed, who ups and leaves.

Before I can react, Duke, Glen and Big Les leap out of their seats towards me. Duke hugs me. 'Now I've heard everything!' he says, releasing me from his grip.

'It's a bloody miracle, son!' says Glen.

'That's what Ellie said this morning,' I say laughing.

Lee Chan bombards his son Sammy in Mandarin, double-checking that he's understood me correctly. Sammy nods, smiles and hugs his dad. Lee approaches me, beaming from ear to ear, his brown eyes bulging. 'Star lucky horse! Chinese, lucky people! Star owners, lucky people too!' he says. Then he bows, stands straight again and meeting my gaze adds, 'I need a whiskey!'

'Order what you like everyone, the drinks are on the house!' I announce.

As Lee Chan makes a beeline to the bar, I feel a tap on my shoulder. I turn around. It's Des, who is beaming from ear to ear. 'It's a miracle, Andy!' he says.

'I know. C'mon mate, let's get ourselves a drink.'

25

★ DES ★

'There you go, Dad.' Marsha places a cup of coffee and a piece of cake down in front of me.

'Thank you,' I say. 'This is a nice surprise.'

She sits down opposite me at a table under a beige sun parasol. We're at a Viennese style café, on the edge of Market Square. It's a sunny, clear day.

'It was pure chance, really. We have a new supplier at work and they just happened to be here in Nottingham. I couldn't have come up here without seeing you, Dad.' I send her a smile and we tuck in to our cakes. 'By the way, thanks for talking to Kyle - you know, about that business with that boy in his class?'

'I'm pleased he felt he could confide in me. Has it helped?'

'It seems to have, yes. He's studying really hard.'

'That's good to hear.'

'I am a bit concerned though.'

'Why's that?'

Marsha plays with the fork on her plate. 'The summer holidays are fast approaching. Six weeks left to his own devices. We'll have one week off together, but the rest of the summer I'm working.'

I see.' I take a sip of my coffee.

'Last summer worked out so well.'

'Didn't you find him a job?'

'Yeah, picking orders in the warehouse. He drove in with me every morning. It gave him a bit of money of his own, you know. But I've checked for vacancies this summer and there's nothing going.'

'Pity.'

'Del is going to take him down to the Job Centre next week, so we'll see.'

'Hopefully something will turn up. When will he find out his exam results?'

'He sits them next week, so in about five weeks' time? I just don't like the idea of him roaming the streets of Birmingham with nothing to do. I just wish he had a couple of friends he could spend time with, but – you know …'

A short silence falls over our table. 'Damn,' I say.

'What is it?'

'I've just realised that I haven't updated him yet. About Star.' I briefly tell Marsha about last night's get together at the King Billy, about Star's set back, her operation and full recovery.

'Wow Dad, that's amazing!'

'It is,' I say.

'Don't worry. Just give Kyle a ring tonight. He'll be so pleased to hear from you.'

* * *

'So she wasn't in any pain, Grandpa?' Kyle says down the

line. I'm stood in the kitchen at home, stirring myself some soup.

'No. I promise. She wasn't in any pain.'

The line goes silent. 'And she's made a full recovery, you say?' Kyle says eventually.

'She has. She's better than ever, according to Andy.' Again, the line goes quiet. 'Kyle?'

'Yeah. I was just thinking. When can I see her?'

'How about next week, the day after your exams? I gave your mum the train money.'

'Thanks Grandpa.'

I pour my soup in to a bowl. 'You're welcome. Just promise me you'll keep your head down till then, yeah?'

'I will. I promise.'

'Good. And best of luck with your exams. Just do your best, alright?'

26

★ ANDY ★

TWELVE HOURS EARLIER

It's gone eleven by the time we spill out of the King Billy, pleasantly inebriated. We say our goodbyes in the pub doorway and head home our separate ways, our hopes and dreams about Star fully restored.

The moment I arrive home my mood changes. I slump on to the sofa and press the button on my answerphone. *You have no new messages,* it answers spitefully. I think about having a beer, but change my mind and pour a Bushmills instead. Reaching for my mobile, I punch in Rita's number. It cuts to voicemail, so I quickly gather my thoughts and speak. 'Hi, it's me. I know I fucked up today - but please allow me the chance to explain. I …' BEEEEPPPP!

There's no time to add any further explanation – and my pride prevents me from leaving a second message. Besides, its late. For a moment I just sit there. Then I down my Bushmills, turn off the living room light and head to bed.

* * *

The following morning, I wake up nursing a sore head. I fumble for my mobile phone and find that the battery's dead. I curse under my breath, stagger into the living room, plug it into the charger, make myself a coffee and then press the power button again. 5%. I check for any left messages. There aren't any. Finishing my coffee, I revert to the landline and dial Ray's number. Star enters my mind and lifts my spirits a little. He picks up.

'Hello Ray, do you have a minute?'

'Sure – how did your news go down with everyone at the pub?'

I smile. 'You should have seen their faces!' Ray laughs down the phone. 'Now everyone is up to speed, I wonder if you'd like to start looking for races for her?'

'Just try stopping me!' says Ray.

* * *

A couple of days pass. Still no word from Rita, but I do get a reply from Ray.

'I've found a race that should be perfect.'

'Where?'

'Under the floodlights at Dunstall Park. Saturday week.'

'Then that's where we'll run.'

'Fingers crossed that the draw is kind to us. We'll not know that until the forty-eight-hour declarations stage. I'll call you when I know.'

'Okay. I'll keep everything crossed.'

* * *

Shortly after Ray's call, I feel strangely deflated. At first, I don't understand why, but slowly the reason comes to me.

While I've nothing against Dunstall Park, Colwick Park had always been my target for Star. That was where I'd had the idea to buy a racehorse in the first place and buying Star had been a decision based upon picking a horse bred to run well there. Star, a horse running in our colours, just up the road at our local racecourse – that had always been the goal. There was another reason why running Star at Colwick Park would have meant so much to me – something to do with mum and dad, though I hadn't been able to identify exactly what these feelings were. Rita would have helped me get to the bottom of that, but she isn't around. And that's when it strikes me, just how much I miss her.

27

★ ANDY ★

The first thing I do when I get home from work, is ring everyone about Star's race at Dunstall Park. Everyone is buzzing at the news. I also tell everyone they'll need to pack overnight cases, as I'll be treating them all to a night at the on-course Holiday Inn. This arrangement suits me as much as anyone else, meaning I can skip an evening's sobriety, not to mention a fifty-mile drive home the same evening. The idea of celebrating Star's win with a can of cola while everyone else is knocking back the beers doesn't hold much appeal.

Before settling down to a quiet evening in front of the TV, I ring the front desk at Dunstall Park Holiday Inn and book four double rooms, including one for Rita and I in the hope that we'll have made our peace by then. I look at my mobile phone out of the corner of my eye but then think again – hoping that all she needs is a little bit more space and time.

* * *

Eight days before the race, Des, Kyle and I drive up to Nine Elms Stables. Ray greets us in the driveway. 'Ellie is over at the stabling area,' he says. 'I just have some admin stuff to see to. As soon as I'm done, I'll join you.' With that he turns around and disappears into the cottage.

We find Ellie in the middle of giving Star a washdown. 'Hi guys,' she says, looking up while spraying Star's hind quarters. 'We're just back from a light workout.' Des prompts Kyle to go and say hello. Ellie smiles as he approaches. 'Good to see you, Kyle,' she says brightly. 'How's things?'

Kyle smiles bashfully. 'Good. A bit tired though. I sat my last GCSE yesterday.'

Ellie smiles. 'How did they go?'

Kyle shrugs. 'It's hard to tell …'

Ellie nods towards Star. 'How about helping me dry her down?'

'Sure.'

Ellie tosses him a spare towel and they set to work. Within a few minutes they're done. Des and I look on as Kyle asks Ellie about Star's eye socket. Kyle is keen to see it. Ellie removes Star's eye patch. 'Do you want to touch it?' asks Ellie.

'Okay.'

We watch as Ellie guides his fingers gently over Star's healed eye socket.

'See?' says Ellie. 'She doesn't feel a thing.'

Kyle looks satisfied. 'No. She doesn't.'

I catch Des' eye. He is doting at Kyle.

'Er, do you want a hand with anything else?' Kyle asks her.

'You can help me muck out her box, if you like?'

'All right,' he says.

Ellie hands me Star's tack. 'Make use of yourself Andy and hold these, will you?'

'Sure,' I say.

Ellie leads Kyle to a shed at the end of the row of horseboxes. Des and I are left alone with Star. Des produces a packet of polos from his pocket. Peeling a couple off the roll, he holds them under Star's mouth. As we watch her guzzling them, Ellie reappears, pushing a large wheelbarrow with Kyle in tow carrying two large spades.

I turn to Des. 'He seems right at home, doesn't he?'

Des smiles. 'Yes, he does.'

Ellie parks the wheelbarrow in the entrance to Star's box and they set to work, shovelling shit. Slowly they fill the wheel barrow. Before long, we're joined by Ray. For a moment, Ray, Des and I idly stand there, watching Ellie and Kyle at work. After a minute or so, Ray turns to Des. 'How old is your grandson, Des?'

'He's sixteen. Why?'

Ray scratches the stubble on his chin. 'Do you think he'd be interested in a summer job?'

I glance at Des. He's struggling to hide his excitement. 'What, here?'

'Yeah, as a stable hand. Mucking out the horses, feeding them, that sort of thing?'

'I reckon he'd jump at the chance.'

Ray says, 'We always take on a couple of extras at this time of the year, you see. And having filled all three places, one of them has just rung and let me down.'

'Perhaps it's best if you speak to Kyle's mum about it?' says Des. He fumbles in his coat pocket and finds a miniature betting shop pen and a screwed-up betting slip. He flattens it out and leans it against my back. 'May I, Andy?'

'Be my guest.'

Des scribbles two telephone numbers onto the betting slip and hands it to Ray. 'These are my daughter's work and home numbers. Her name is Marsha. I'm sure she'll be very pleased to hear from you.'

'Okay,' says Ray. 'I'll have a chat with Ellie and ask her to give Marsha a ring.'

I look at Des. He's beaming with pride. He sends me a smile and I give him a discreet thumbs up sign.

* * *

With Star's box clean and laid with a bed of fresh hay, Ray takes her reigns and leads her into the box. Ellie and Kyle brush themselves down, a job well done. Ellie turns to Kyle.

'How about a can of cola and a snack for your troubles?'

Kyles smiles awkwardly. 'Er, do you have any Fanta?'

Ellie says, 'As a matter of fact, I do.'

'Great!' says Kyle. And with that, we all head back towards the cottage.

As we arrive, the sun comes out. Ellie heads inside and returns with two cans of Fanta and a couple of hi-fibre bars. She sits down beside Kyle on a bench in front of the cottage and they set about their snacks. Meanwhile, Ray leads Des and I into his office. He invites us to sit down opposite him at his desk.

'Okay, so do either of you know who the leading jockey is at Dunstall Park this season?' he says. I give him a blank look. 'Des?'

'Seb Sanders?'

'Correct,' says Ray.

Des goes on. 'He's the current Champion Apprentice jockey, isn't he?'

'Yes, he is – and he boasts a twenty four percent strike

rate at Dunstall Park this season. Now Seb's agent and I go way back and I'm happy to tell you that through him, I've managed to secure Seb's services for the ride on Star.' I can't help but feel impressed. Ray goes on. 'Now, a few days before Star was due to run at Colwick Park, do you recall I worked her with another horse?'

Des and I nod simultaneously.

'Well yesterday, Ellie and I did something similar. We ran her on the oval all-weather gallop with a horse called Billy's Secret. Like Star, he also likes left-handed oval tracks. We loaded them both in the gate like it were a proper race - Ellie on Star in box one and Colin on Billy in box two, you know, the apprentice we used at Southwell on her debut.'

I say, 'How did it go?'

Ray smiles. 'Like clockwork.'

'Really?' says Des.

Ray nods. 'When the gate sprung open, Star jumped out in a flash. Now Billy's Secret is no slouch in starting his races, but Star was away like lightning. She made the inside rail her own and by the time she turned into the bend she'd put two lengths between her and Billy. Then she straightened up for home and pulled away. Ellie rode her out to the line. She "won" comfortably by over three lengths.'

'Blimey,' I say.

Des says, 'How good is this Billy's Secret?'

Ray smiles. 'He won off a mark of seventy at Southwell last week. To put that run into perspective, Star will run off a mark of sixty on Saturday night, the rating she was allocated back in May.' I turn to Des and smile. He beams back at me. Ray continues, 'Neither of you need to be Einstein to know that Star is a "good thing" on Saturday night.'

Des isn't yet satisfied. 'This Colin. Was he flat out on Billy's Secret?'

'Flat to the boards,' says Ray. Finally, Des appears convinced. He looks at me. I look at Ray. Further words aren't necessary, though Ray hammers the message home. 'Just be sure that you all have a proper bet on Saturday.'

'We will, Ray' I say. 'Trust me.'

'Good,' he says. 'Because you'll never get another opportunity quite like it – not after the handicapper has her reassessed.'

* * *

When we arrive outside, we find Ellie and Kyle sitting in the sunshine together. She's showing Kyle how to tighten a horse's bridle. For a moment, the three of us stand in an informal circle outside the cottage in blissful silence, enjoying the weather.

Ray says, 'oh yeah, before I forget – Ellie here has some exciting news to share, don't you?'

Ellie hands Kyle the bridle, gets to her feet and joins us. 'Ray's asked me to consider becoming his apprentice jockey.'

'Bloody hell,' I say. 'That's great news!'

Des smiles broadly. 'Congratulations, young lady. I hope you're going to accept?'

Ellie blushes. 'Yes – at least, I'm seriously considering it.'

'As you've seen for yourselves, Ellie has loads of natural ability,' says Ray. 'And her seven-pound claim will come in really handy, particularly with a stable full of handicappers like mine.'

'What a pity you don't already have your licence,' says Des.

'Ellie smiles. 'How do you mean?'

'Because if you ask me, there's no one better qualified to ride Star on Saturday night than you.'

Ellie blushes. 'I'm not sure that's true, but thanks for the vote of confidence.'

'You're welcome.' Des turns to Ray. 'I hope Seb Sanders listens closely to your instructions on Saturday, Ray?'

'Oh, he will. Don't you worry about that!'

28

★ MARSHA ★

'Is that Marsha James?'

'Speaking.'

'This is Ellie Mc Govern. I work at Nine Elms Stables?' I unlock the front door to the house and enter. 'Your dad is a co-owner of one of the horses we have in training?'

'You're talking about Star?' I say.

'That's right,' says the voice at the other end of the line. I enter the living room and sit down in my favourite armchair. Ellie goes on. 'As you know, Des and Kyle were up here yesterday.'

'That's right. Kyle has talked of nothing since! What can I do for you, Ellie?'

'Do you have a minute?'

'Sure.'

'Okay. Well, it's like this, see. Ray, that's my boss, thought I should have a private word with you first.'

'He's not caused any trouble, has he?' I say.

Ellie laughs. 'God no – quite the contrary. You see, Ray would like to offer him a summer job.'

'Pardon?'

'Well, a fortnight's trial. Just to see how he gets on.' My eyes well up. 'Ray and I both find him so positive and he seems very comfortable around the yard. Yesterday he helped me wash Star down and muck out her box. He was asking me about bridles and all sorts. We think he'd be a natural fit here.' A tear rolls down my cheek as Ellie continues. 'He shows a lot more initiative than many of the ones we've employed here before. So, if he is keen, we're happy to give him the chance. We have a vacancy here at short notice, you see.' I'm speechless. 'Marsha?'

'Yes. Er, sorry. It's just so nice to receive such positive feedback about my son. He's had a tough time of it. School and that.' The line goes quiet for a moment. 'The thing is we live in Birmingham. If Kyle is keen, how would that work?'

'Accommodation is provided,' says Ellie. 'We have a self-contained cottage on site for stable hands.'

'I see.'

'So, what do you think?'

'Kyle has never lived away from home before. He also has one or two issues, mostly to do with food.'

'There are plenty of us here to keep an eye on him,' Ellie says. 'And you'd be welcome to drop by, or stay over if you felt like it. I live on site, too - and there are two horse mad girls around Kyle's age who worked here last summer, who will be back again this year.'

'It sounds perfect,' I say.

'Ray pays competitive rates and if the trial goes okay, the job is his for the summer. We're flexible about hours, although he would be expected to work most of the weekends, given the amount of racing there is at this time of the year.'

'So, ', I say. 'Shall I have a chat with him?'

'Yeah, great. Tell him that the work trial is his if he'd like it. The only thing is that we'll need his decision soon. Sorry it's such short notice. As I say, we've been let down at the last minute. He'd be expected to start in the middle of next week.'

'All right. Well, thanks for the call, Ellie. Kyle or I will ring you back tomorrow.'

'Good. And thank *you,* Marsha. Kyle would be very welcome here.' With that she rings off.

I walk out into the hall way and call out up the stair case. 'Kyle, love. Can I have a word?'

'Coming,' shouts Kyle from upstairs.

* * *

We sit down in the living room together and I explain about the call I've just received. When I'm finished, I look him in the eyes. 'So, are you keen to try it out, love?'

'You bet!'

'See how you get on, yeah?'

'Yeah. I'll see how it goes.'

I hand him a scrap of paper. 'Here is Ellie's number. Maybe you'd prefer to sleep on it? Give her your decision in the morning?'

'No, Mum. I'm certain. I'll ring Ellie now. Then I'll ring Grandpa and after that I'll ring dad.'

As I look at him, a funny thing happens. The troubled looking boy I've become so used to, struggling under the weight of a headful of questions from his school psychologist, is suddenly nowhere to be seen. A tear rolls down my cheek. Kyle sends me a confused look.

'Why are you crying?', he says. 'Are you sad?'

'No love, I'm not sad. Quite the opposite. I'm crying because I'm happy.'

Kyle gets out of his chair and sits himself down beside me. I pull him close and ruffle his hair and this time, he doesn't push my hand away.

29

★ SHIRELLE JAMES ★

SIX YEARS EARLIER, GOLD CUP DAY, MARCH, 1991

'Something smells good in there, Shirelle. Are you cooking what I think you're cooking?'

I turn around and there he is, stood in the kitchen door way in his bus driver's uniform holding a bouquet of flowers. He smiles and holds it out towards me. I walk across the kitchen and give him a kiss.

'Thank you, Desmond and yes - I've made Bajan Fish Stew.' Everyone calls him Des, but to me, he will always be Desmond. He holds me tightly and nuzzles my neck. 'Stop it,' I say, smiling. 'You've got cold hands!'

'It's November in Nottingham, woman,' he says, joining in my laughter, 'and I need warming up!'

I wriggle free. 'I can taste rum on your lips.' He smiles back at me and raises an eyebrow. 'You're not going to tell me he went and won, are you?' I say.

For a moment he just stands there, milking the moment. 'What have I been saying about Garrison Savannah for some time now?'

'That he's a Gold Cup winner in the making?'

'Exactly,' says Desmond. 'And today, he became one!'

'No!' I hug him tightly.

'At odds of 16/1, no less!'

'You're joking?' I laugh.

'No, it's true!' He lifts me off my feet and swings me around. 'Just before the off, I convinced Duke to back him too. He insisted on buying me a couple of Cockspurs at the King Billy. I never realised Pat had such good rum down there!'

He fetches his work bag from where he left it, just inside the kitchen door. He lifts it on the kitchen table and tips it open. Several tightly rolled bundles of banknotes roll out across the table. One or two of them drop to the floor. I hold my hand to my mouth. 'How much did you win?'

'Over half of what we need. And I have a plan for how we win the rest.'

* * *

A short while later, we're sat in the living room eating our supper. Des takes a swig of beer and looks across the table at me. For some reason, he begins talking about holidays. Perhaps it's because of the cold weather outside. 'Remember our first holiday abroad after moving here?'

'Of course?' I say. 'A week on the Costa Blanca!' Desmond looks up from his fish stew and smiles. I take a sip of red wine. 'I shall never forget how good it felt, dipping my toes in to the Mediterranean Sea for the first time.'

'Me neither,' says Desmond. 'I think we spent every day on that beach. Sometimes, while you were busy building sand castles with Marsha, I would close my eyes and imagine we were back on Pebbles Beach.' I reach my hand across the table and gives his hand an affectionate squeeze. 'I remember what fun I had, during the build-up to that holiday - sneaking downstairs to check the post each morning before you were up, determined to keep it a surprise from you.'

'I remember,' I say, smiling.

'When the envelope from Cosmos Holidays finally arrived, I slipped it onto your breakfast tray which I served to you at this very table.'

'Yes, you did!'

Desmond laughs. 'It wasn't easy, getting Marsha her first passport on the quiet and making sure ours were up to date without you noticing.'

I glance out of the window and smile. 'I shall never forget. You told me we had a very nice man called Noel Murless to thank for making that holiday possible.'

Desmond laughs so hard he almost chokes on his beer. 'That's right! You thought Noel Murless must have been my boss at the bus company!'

I put down my wine glass and join in his laughter. 'Well how was I to know that he was the man who trained Royal Palace to win the 1967 Derby? I knew even less about racing in those days than I do now!'

Desmond looks at me pensively. 'I'm not sure I ever told you how much I had on Royal Palace that day.'

'I wouldn't have wanted to have known either,' I say. A short silence falls over the table.

'Package holidays weren't so expensive in those days,' he says. 'Quite different to trying to get the money together for a holiday in Barbados.'

* * *

The racehorse Garrison Savannah first entered our lives four years earlier, one cold, Saturday October morning. Desmond and I were sitting in the living room together reading the papers. Suddenly he looks up at me from his Mirror Racing supplement. 'Well would you believe it?' he says, walking over to where I'm sitting. Handing me the racing page, he says, 'read back to me the names of the runners in today's four o' clock at Sandown Park.'

I do as he asks. 'Daybrook's Gift, Harbour Girl …' The name of the next horse jumps off the page at me. 'Garrison Savannah.' I never shared Desmond's passion for racing, but after discovering that there was a horse running that afternoon whose name meant so much to us, Jenny Pitman's Bay provided us with a common interest. That afternoon, Desmond put some money on him at the betting shop at the end of our road. He finished sixth - but just three weeks later he won a hurdle race at Worcester at odds of 9/1. Desmond bet on him and we won a ninety pounds. So taken was he by the manner of his win – 'it was a whole twenty-two lengths back to the third placed horse, Shirelle!' – that that afternoon, he came up with an idea. It came to him on his way home from the betting shop, his pockets jingling with our winnings. He said, 'You know how fond the British are of their Bank holidays?' I nodded. 'Well as of today, I would like to propose a new Bank Holiday, a very special one, just for you and me.'

'How do you mean?' I was intrigued.

'What I'm suggesting is this. From today onwards, whenever Garrison Savannah runs, we commemorate the occasion by having a Bajan supper, a bottle of wine and an evening looking through our old photo albums of home. We'll call it "Garrison Savannah Day" - our very *own* Bank Holiday. What do you think?'

Of course, I loved the idea – and between Garrison Savannah's win that afternoon in 1987 and his victory in the Gold Cup four years later, Desmond and I enjoyed no less than thirteen such 'Bank Holidays' of our own. More than often, Garrison Savannah ran at the big Saturday meetings, a day on which we were usually both free. We would watch his races together, while enjoying a glass of wine or a beer and some snacks in front of the telly and afterwards, prepare some Bajan dish or other together. Desmond began saving the money he won backing him and following his win in the Gold Cup, we'd accrued a tidy sum.

* * *

Three weeks after winning the Gold Cup, it was time for another 'Garrison Savannah Day' when he lined up in the 1991 Grand National at Aintree. Though Desmond didn't say exactly how much he was going to have on him, I had a pretty good idea. Desmond was a gambler and by no means a bad one, but he was also a romantic - so I knew he'd most likely go 'all in.' It therefore stood to reason that if Garrison Savannah won the big race at Aintree that afternoon, we'd all be off to Barbados later in the year.

* * *

An hour before the race, I watch him, stood in the hallway, fetching his pork-pie hat and wrapping his scarf around his neck. 'Why not come to the bookies and watch the race with me?' he says. He knew I'd say no, of course – and I suspected the reason he was going to watch the race at the bookies was because he felt too nervous to watch the race with me.

'I'm fine here, Desmond,' I say, adjusting his scarf. 'Besides, someone has to prepare the Pudding and Souse!' I kiss him on the door step. 'Ring me after the race, okay?'

'Okay, love.'

'And Desmond?'

'Yes, love?'

'I'll keep everything crossed.'

'Bye, love,' he says, his smile failing to disguise his nerves.

* * *

Fast forward a few months. As I reach the beach, I stop in my tracks and take off my sandals. Though the sun is hot, there's a lovely, gentle breeze. I feel the baking sand between my toes. I look up and smile. The sky is bright blue and there isn't a cloud in sight. I sigh contentedly to myself and set off across the beach towards the sea. A little further on I take a look around, stop and unfold the deck chairs I'm carrying. They're the old-fashioned type, the ones with red and white striped canvas backs. I sit down, bury my toes in the sand and close my eyes. Seagulls swirl above my head. The sound of the tides ebb and flow sooths my mind. I open my eyes and look straight ahead. Nothing but sky, sea and sand. *Wonderful.*

I hear Desmond's voice call out from somewhere behind me. I turn around and there he is, trudging across the beach, smiling and waving. He's soon just a couple of feet away.

'You'll never guess what?' he says.

I hold my hand to my face to shield my eyes from the sun. 'What?'

'There was a vendor selling cold drinks on the promenade.' I squint back at him and smile. 'So, I bought a bottle of soda and two bottles of beer. I forgot to ask what you'd like so I bought both. Sorry, I must be getting old,' he laughs.

'You and me both, Desmond.' I take the bottle of cold soda and make a gesture for him to sit down beside me.

* * *

It was true. Old age was creeping up on the both of us. Desmond turned sixty last week and I wasn't far behind. He sits down beside me, with a bottle of beer in each hand. I look at him and then at the bottles.

'What?' he says.

'That worked out well,' I say, my eyes dancing with mischief. I laugh and Desmond joins in. We take a swig from our drinks. 'How do you like the spot I picked?'

He looks around and smiles. 'It's perfect. It's as though we have the whole beach to ourselves.'

'That's what I thought.' I feel for Desmond's hand on his arm rest. He takes it.

'You, me, the sun and the sea. Sometimes, I don't want for anything else.'

I feel him squeeze my hand gently. 'Me neither.'

A short silence falls over us. All that can be heard is the sound of the gulls and the waves, coming in from the English Channel. It's Desmond who speaks next.

'They may not bathe horses in the sea here, Shirelle, like at home. But I'm really glad we decided to get away for a few days.'

'Me too, Desmond,' I say. 'Me too.'

* * *

The following day, our train crosses the county border back into Nottinghamshire. I look at him sat in the window seat opposite. 'There's something I need you to promise me.'

He looks up from his newspaper. 'Of course. Anything.'

'Never stop trying, will you?'

'How do you mean?'

'What I mean is … should I pass away before you, never give up on our dream. Of taking Marsha and Kyle to Barbados.'

'Don't talk like that, Shirelle. When I win enough money, you'll be on that plane too!'

'I'm just saying, that's all. Will you promise me?'

His eyes meet mine. 'I promise.'

'Good.'

I look at him and smile. And wipe away the tear that rolls down my cheek before he sees it.

* * *

Two weeks before Garrison Savannah was beaten into second place by Seagram in the Grand National, I receive a letter from Nottingham University Hospital, providing me with the results of what I understood to be some routine tests. Instead, the letter urged me to return for an emergency appointment the following Monday morning. That was the day I was told I only had a few months to live. I always meant to buck up the courage to tell Desmond, but I could never quite bring myself to do it. Before I knew it, the Grand National was upon us.

Around five minutes after the race, the telephone rings. I pick up. *Beep, beep, beep, beep.* I'm connected, though the line remains silent. 'Desmond?' More silence. Eventually he answers.

'I'm sorry, Shirelle.'

'Don't be,' I say.

'The second time, coming around the elbow, when he took the lead …'

'Desmond -'

'Three, four lengths clear …'

'I know.'

The line goes silent again, before his voice returns. 'For a moment it was real. I saw us all sat on the plane, Barbados down below, preparing to land.' His voice gives way to muffled tears.

'He gave his all.' I say.

'Yes, he did. He didn't have anything left to give.'

Silence. 'Come home, Desmond.' There follows a long silence. 'Desmond?'

'All right,' he sighs.

'The Pudding and Souse, it's soon ready. And win or lose, it's still "Garrison Savannah Day" isn't it?'

30

★ ANDY ★

I wake in darkness soaked in sweat. It was the same last night and the night before that, with the last words Rita said to me, ringing in my ears. *'Don't get in touch unless you're serious about being a part of our baby's life!'* I switch on my bedside lamp and check the time. Three-fifty-five. The alarm is due to ring at four, so I switch it off and drag myself out of bed. *How am I supposed to reassure her I'm serious if she won't return my calls?* I head to the bathroom for a shower. Ten minutes later I dress, skip my morning coffee and head off to work.

* * *

Early afternoon, my postal delivery complete, I clock out and cycle home. As I step into the hallway, the telephone starts ringing. I run into the living room and lunge for the phone.

'Rita?'

'Andy, it's Ray.'

'Hello Ray.'

'I bear good news. Lady Luck is shining down on you.'

'How do you mean?'

'The forty-eight-hour declarations have been made and I've just received a fax from Weatherby's. Star has been drawn in stall two.'

'That's excellent news.'

'It is, though I reckon you've all been due a bit of luck.'

'While you're on Ray, what time is she running?'

'Race two, at six-thirty.'

* * *

Within minutes of talking with Ray, my anxiety about Rita returns. I head to the kitchen, open the window wide open and light a cigarette. I think about driving to her work in Basford. Or perhaps first I should drop by her flat? I stub out my cigarette and return to the sofa in the living room and stare at the telephone. I rehearse a variety of brief messages out loud, pick up the receiver and punch in her number. It cuts directly to answerphone.

'Hello Rita – I know you probably still think I'm a total shit, but the reason I was late was because' - BEEEEPPPP!

'Shit!' I hang up, re-dial and try again. 'Because a miracle has happened and Star is better than ever and' – BEEEPPPP!

'For fuck's sake!'

I take a deep breath, exhale slowly and repeat the process. 'StarisrunningonSaturdaynightanditseemsmeaninglessun-lessyou're' – BEEEPPP!

'Andy?' I hear Rita's voice. I almost jump out of my skin. I turn around and there she is, stood like a ghost in the living room doorway.

'Bloody hell! You almost gave me a heart …' My words tail off as I look at her, all puffy faced and raw red eyes. Her tummy bump has come on fiercely.

'Sorry I startled you. I knocked on the front door, but I don't think you …'

She starts crying. I walk towards her and stop a few steps in front of her. Then she throws herself at me and begins bawling her eyes out.

* * *

A few minutes later, we're sat opposite one another in the living room, with a giant mug of tea each. Rita is biting her nails. Her nervousness is contagious.

'Rita, listen. While I may have some fears about becoming a -'

She cuts me short. 'Sorry. Before you say anything, there's something I need to get off my chest.'

'Oh, right,' I say. 'Go ahead.'

She takes a deep breath and then slowly exhales. 'Do you remember that time, ages ago, when we told one another about significant ex's from our pasts?'

'Yeah, I do. I told you about a girl called Beth.'

'That's right. And I told you about somebody called Eric?'

'Yes. I remember.' A wave of paranoia engulfs me. 'This isn't where you tell me that you're getting back together with him, is it?'

'God no,' she says. She manages a tiny smile before continuing. 'It's just that I never really gave you the full story about our relationship and, well - it's high time that I did.'

* * *

My mouth feels dry. I shuffle in my seat. All Rita had told me about Eric was that he was a foreign student from Switzerland who she'd dated at uni. Perhaps it was jealousy on my part, but I'd never liked the sound of him. When she later told me that he started going to the City Ground to watch Forest during his second year, I knew my instincts about him had been right all along. Rita cups her mug in her hands and begins. 'At the beginning of my third year, I missed my period. I took a pregnancy test. It was positive.' Rita throws me a quick glance.

'Blimey.' I nod to her to carry on.

'Eric seemed as happy as I was, despite the tricky timing. But slowly his feelings seemed to change. As his finals approached – he was in the year above me - we began rowing. I think he felt a huge pressure to get a good degree, but his growing ambiguity towards our relationship made me anxious. I was allocated a mid-wife and a date for our first ultra-sound was set. Everything between us seemed to be coming to a head. I ended up telling him that unless he was at the clinic for the ultra-sound appointment, I would assume that we no longer had a future together, which would force me to take matters into my own hands.'

'What, like, have an abortion?'

She nods. 'Needless to say, he never showed. A few days later I terminated the pregnancy. The following week I called by his flat. It didn't surprise me to find that it was empty. I guess he'd run away back to Zurich.' Slowly her tears fall. 'When you didn't show the other day, all this stuff flooded back.' She reaches for a packet of tissues in her handbag and taking one, blows her nose. I get up and sit down beside her and gently stroke her hair. We remain like this for a while.

'If I'd had any idea about this, you know, *before.* I'm so sorry, Rita.'

She wipes her eyes again. 'Knowing you, you'd still have been bloody late!' she laughs.

I find myself joining in. 'I'll let you have that one,' I say smiling.

She looks at me, all puffy eyed and blotchy cheeks. 'I'm joking. How were you to know about any of this?' Rita falls silent for a moment. 'In the days that followed after the abortion, I swore to myself that should I ever get pregnant again, things would be different. At the same time, I'm sorry – because in many ways, you were the victim of the treatment I never got to dish out to Eric.' For a moment we just sit there while our teas go cold.

'Something has just occurred to me.'

'What?' she says.

'This is the first time since you told me you were pregnant that you've appeared, well, vulnerable.'

She looks at me. 'Is that a bad thing?'

'No. Quite the contrary. It's very human. These past few days while you haven't been around, has made me realise that I want this child just as much as you do. But that isn't to say that I haven't had my doubts over the past few months about how I'll do, you know, as a dad. Whether or not I'll cut it as–'

Rita cuts me short. 'Don't you think I haven't had similar fears too?'

For a while I remain silent. 'I guess.'

'Besides. You'll be a great dad.'

'You think?'

'I know,' she says.

I reach in and kiss her. 'I have something to show you,' I say. I hold out my hand. Slowly, she takes it. 'Follow me.' I lead her in silence towards the bedroom and stop in front of the closed door. 'Cover your eyes,' I say.

She looks at me. 'What?'

'Please. Just do as I ask.' She closes her eyes. 'Are they closed tightly?' I say.

'Yes.'

'Good.' Taking her hand, I open the door and lead her to the foot of my bed. 'Okay,' I say.

'Open them.' She opens her eyes and beside my bed sees the baby cot, the one she fell in love with at the store when we were up in town together.

* * *

'Are you hungry?' says Rita. It's early evening the same day.

'I am a bit, yeah. What are you in the mood for?'

She thinks for a moment. 'Pizza with extra cheese and pepperoni.'

'Then that's what we'll have.' With that, I phone our favourite pizza delivery place in Hockley.

Eating our pizzas, I finally I get the chance to tell her all about my afternoon at Nine Elms Stables, Star's complete transformation and her up and coming race at Dunstall Park – not to mention our 'night over' at the Holiday Inn the night after next. I turn and look at her. 'You will come, won't you? It wouldn't be the same, seeing Star run without –'

She cuts me short. 'Of course I'll come.'

'Good.' A short silence falls over us. It's Rita who breaks it.

'Something's just occurred to me.'

'What's that?'

'That we haven't actually shared our big news with anyone yet,' she says, tapping her tummy.

31

★ ANDY ★

It's the day of the race and Rita and I are running late. As we head along Sneinton Dale and turn the corner onto Manvers Road, I see them all ahead, chatting and laughing, congregated on the street beside the white Transit van.

'Here they are!' says Big Les, pointing at us.

'Better late than never!' jokes Duke.

'Sorry,' I say, red-faced.

'It's my fault,' says Rita, breathlessly. 'I couldn't find my heels. I bought them especially.'

'I took the liberty of fetching these, Andy,' says Glen, holding up the keys to the van.

* * *

I barely recognise the motley crew stood before me. Everyone is suited, booted and have scrubbed up nicely, not least Des, who's wearing a stylish flat cap in place of his usual pork pie one. 'All set?' I say.

Everyone nods.

'Okay, good.' I glance at Rita, who sends me a smile and nods. 'So, before we head off to Wolverhampton, Rita and I would just like to –'

Sammy Chan smiles cheekily. 'Share some good news?'

'Er, yeah - exactly.'

Duke steps forward. 'Sneinton's worst kept secret is about to be revealed!' He then turns to Rita and kisses her on the cheek.

'Is it *that* obvious?' she says, stroking her tummy.

'Pretty much!' says Glen, with a wink of the eye.

Duke gives me a hug. 'Congratulations!'

'Thanks Duke,' I say, laughing.

Glen produces a small bouquet of flowers that he'd concealed behind his back. He hands them to Rita and kisses her on the cheek. 'Congratulations, young lady!'

'They're beautiful. Thank you, Glen.'

'It couldn't have happened to a nicer couple,' he says. Rita hugs him tightly. Glen had been like a father-figure to Rita when she worked at the bookies.

'We thought it only wise to wait, you see, until after the ultra-scan results before – you know, saying anything,' says Rita. 'That was two weeks ago - but with so much else going on with Star …'

I put my arm around her shoulder. 'We are happy to tell you that our baby looks healthy and well.' Everyone cheers and claps. I look at my watch. 'So – is everyone ready for the Black Country?'

* * *

Rita sits in the front of the transit van between Des and I. A few miles out of Nottingham, Des has some exciting news of his own to share. 'You'll never guess?'

'What?' says Rita.

'Ray's offered Kyle a two-week trial as a stable hand.'

I look at Des. He's beaming from ear-to-ear. 'I take it he's said yes?' I say.

Des nods. 'He starts next Wednesday.'

Rita squeezes his arm. 'You must be one proud Grandpa?'

'Thank you, Rita,' he says. 'I am.'

* * *

Just over halfway to Wolverhampton, Rita nudges me. 'Can we make a toilet stop?'

'Sure. I'll pull over into the next service station.' A few minutes later, I park up in the forecourt of a Happy Chef Restaurant. 'Coffee break, Lads,' I announce. Everyone hops out and stretches their legs. 'Can I order you something, while you're in the Ladies?'

'I have a craving for a vanilla milkshake – but any flavour will do.'

* * *

Rita's need for the toilet provides Duke and I with a chance to refresh everybody's minds about the betting coup. It's the same plan as the one we'd devised for the race that never was at Colwick Park, three months ago. As everyone takes a seat inside the Happy Chef with their refreshments, Duke removes a wad of photocopies of Wolverhampton town centre from his inner suit pocket. The maps are divided into four sections. They're colour coded, just as before. As Rita joins us and makes a start on her milkshake, I get the ball rolling. Duke holds up one of the maps and I point at it with a white plastic straw. 'Big Les and Duke have the bookies in the blue section, Des and One-Armed the ones in the green section, Rita and I have the red section and Sammy and Lee the yellow one. We have four betting shops each.'

Duke takes over. 'We have thirty minutes to get as many bets on Star as possible. Remember, a maximum of a tenner per slip, a maximum of twenty slips per person. S.P. only, no early bird prices. I wouldn't put anyone off doing some combination forecast and tricast bets as well, as well as each-way Lucky Fifteens with other horses you fancy. Any questions?'

I notice One-Armed make to say something. 'One-Armed?'

'I just wondered if … Nah. Never mind.'

Sammy pipes up. 'What's Star's race card number?'

'Good question,' I say.

Lee Chan checks in his Racing Post. 'Number four.'

Duke nods. 'Er, anything else?'

I look at One-Armed. He looks away. Duke says, 'Everyone clear about the plan?'

A murmur of agreement sweeps around the table and as soon as we've finished our snacks, we head straight back to the van.

* * *

Upon arriving in Wolverhampton, I follow the signs for the Mander Shopping Centre car park in the heart of the town centre. After parking, Rita, Des and I climb out of the drivers compartment.

'I feel a bit woozy,' says Rita.

'Why not find somewhere to sit down and rest? I'll put our bets on.'

'Are you sure?'

'Of course.'

With Rita resting up at a café, at the stroke of midday, the rest of us infiltrate Wolverhampton's betting shop fraternity with military efficiency. We reconvene thirty minutes later, our bets placed. After collecting Rita, who looks decidedly perkier after another milkshake, we head to The Wheatsheaf pub on nearby Market Street for a pub lunch. Inside, everyone eagerly compares bets. A couple of pints later, we stroll back to The Mander Shopping centre car park, a plan well executed and continue our journey to the racecourse.

32

★ ANDY ★

At just after four o 'clock, I drive through the gates to Dunstall Park Racecourse. After parking the van, the nine of us head straight for the Holiday Inn Hotel, situated adjacent to the astro-turf like green parade ring. As I check everyone in at reception, Des points at a poster on the wall.

'Look! A Tom Jones impersonator is doing a set after racing!'

The poster shows a chubby, medallioned, middle-aged man dressed in a frilly white shirt, open to his waist, wearing a pair of skin tight black trousers.

Big Les studies the poster. 'He looks more like Jimmy Tarbuck, if you ask me!' Duke and One-Armed laugh out loud.

* * *

We make arrangements to meet in the hotel bar at five, one hour before the first race.

Rita and I have a room on the second floor. I open the

door with my card key and we enter. The rooms interior is an unusual mix of lime green, beige and brown.

'I think I'll take forty winks,' she says.

I give her a cuddle in the entrance to the bedroom. 'Sure,' I say, planting a kiss on her forehead. I walk to the bedroom window and draw the curtains. Before doing so, I look out over the parade ring. Slowly but surely, the Saturday crowd are beginning to arrive. A pang of excitement surges through me, when I think of Star's date with destiny in less than two hours' time.

* * *

At shortly after five, the nine of us gather in the hotel lounge bar. Rita looks a picture of pregnant good health and spirits are running high. The atmosphere in the bar is boisterous but friendly. Duke discreetly points out a couple of West Midlands trainers with roguish reputations – all fat cigars, chunky spirit glasses and shiny suits. We watch as one of them tips his owners a horse at an away meeting. They follow the race live up on the big screen. Cheers ring out from their table as the horse obliges.

I finish my beer and turn to Duke. 'How about we drop by the betting ring ahead of the first? See how many bookmakers are along the rails?'

'Good idea,' he says, downing the final dregs of his pint.

Rita turns to me. 'I thought of heading up to the hospitality box until Star's race?'

'Good idea.' I give her a kiss. 'See you in the parade ring just after six, yeah?'

Rita nods, smiles and heads towards the grandstand foyer.

* * *

Duke, Big Les, Des, Glen, The Chans, One-Armed and I arrive in the betting ring. As the runners for the opening handicap canter down to the one-mile start, betting in the ring is lively. I take a look around. There's a decent crowd: a mixture of Saturday night good time seekers, chancers and racing aficionados. Duke removes a cigarillo from his carton and lights one, before nodding discreetly at the front row of bookmaker's pitches along the rails. 'That's where we should chance our luck later.' I nod in agreement.

'And they're racing in the opener at Wolverhampton!' announces the racecourse commentator Derek 'Tommo' Thompson over the tannoy. None of us bother with a bet in the first race.

I turn to everyone. 'How about we head to the Parade Ring?' Seven faces nod back at me and with that, we head off to catch up with Ray and Ellie.

* * *

After showing our owners' badges at the entrance, we're ushered inside. Rita has already arrived and is sharing a joke with Ray. I've never seen Ray so clean shaven.

'Andy,' he says, shaking my hand. 'Hello everyone!' he adds, turning to address the rest of the group. We gather in an informal semi-circle around him and greetings and hand-shakes are exchanged. 'Look,' he says, pointing. 'Here they come.'

Ellie proudly leads Star past. She acknowledges Rita and I with an excited smile. My confidence in Star's chances increase when I look at her. Her coat has a shiny gleam to it, like velvet. Everything about her demeanour radiates good health and wellbeing. Her hind legs look supple and muscular and there isn't an ounce of fat on her smooth, streamlined body. The yellow head gear she wore when burning up the gallops when I mistook her for another horse is on. So taken am I by her appearance, I don't notice our jockey enter the fray. Suddenly stood before me is Seb Sanders, resplendent in our red and green silks.

'Evening all!' he says in a jovial brummie accent.

'Hello, Seb,' come a chorus of replies.

Everyone takes turns to shake his hand. Seb Sanders resembles the human equivalent of Star – compact, muscular and evidently in tip top physical condition. Ray sidles over to him. 'A quick word if I may, Seb?'

* * *

I look at my watch. It's twelve minutes past six. A wave of butterflies flutter in my stomach. I try to ignore them and turn to my friends. 'C'mon, fellas. It's time.'

We head towards the parade ring exit. As I follow the others through the partition, something makes me turnaround. I look back just in time to see Ray giving Seb the leg up on to Star. My eyes follow Seb and Star as they calmly make their way along the racecourse chute, before disappearing out of sight.

'Nervous?' says Rita.

'Very nervous. But proud too.'

'So you should be.' She caresses my arm. 'See you soon up in the box, yeah?'

'Sure. As soon as our money's on, I'll join you.'

'Great. And Andy?'

'Yes?'

'It's exciting, isn't it?'

I look at her again, smile and give her a kiss. For a

moment my nerves subside. 'It is. Ten months work in the making.'

I hear a voice calling my name. It belongs to Big Les. 'Hurry up, Andy! We'll miss the best odds!'

* * *

As we enter the betting ring, the floodlights come on. The weird mixture of daylight and artificial light throws a surreal colour cast across people's faces. Arriving at the rail pitches, we blend in with the front line of punters. Duke is stood beside me. The butterflies in my stomach intensify. I glance at my watch. Six-eighteen. The bookmaker on the number one pitch, a giant of a man with a bull dog like face, starts over from the top.

'2/1 Delquay, 3/1 Brave Emperor, 9/2 Lunar Ocean, 7/1 bar!'

I turn and face Duke. 'Shall I ask what price he has about Star?'

Duke takes out his miniature cigars and lights one. 'Not yet, Andy. Glen?'

'Yeah?'

Duke points to some nearby pitches away from the rails. 'Go and see what price those fellas are offering about Star on their boards.'

A moment later, Glen's back. 'She's 25's all along the line.'

'A bit short, isn't she?' I say.

Duke nods. 'Let's keep our paint dry for another minute or two. She's sure to drift,' he adds. 'The first three in the betting all come from fancy Newmarket yards. It's my guess most of the money will be for them, when it arrives. That ought to push everything else out.'

A stony-faced bookmaker on pitch number two looks as though he's keen to get some money into his book. '9/4 Delquay,' he shouts, '11/4 Brave Emperor, 5/1 Lunar Ocean, 15/2 bar!' The changes at the head of the market trigger a flurry of activity around his joint. Punters' jostle past us, keen to 'get on'. Everywhere one looks, bets are being placed, laid and hedged.

Duke nudges me. 'Okay everybody,' I say. 'It's time to strike.' We fan out along the rails. I take out a cigarette, light it and head straight for the 'Bull Dog' on pitch one. 'What price number four?'

The Bull-Dog raises an eyebrow. 'Manvers Road Star?'

'Yeah,' I say, peeling the notes off a roll of fifties, puffing on my cigarette.

'33's,' he barks.

'Okay. I'll have two hundred and fifty each way.'

The Bull Dog shoots me a wary look. My mobile starts buzzing in my pocket. With a 'monkey' in my right hand and my mobile in my left, Rita's number blinks on the screen. I tap accept call.

'Andy!'

The phone reception is poor. 'Rita?'

'My contractions have started!'

'What?' I say.

The Bull-Dog growls. 'Are you having a bet or what?'

'My contractions,' Rita repeats. 'They've started!'

33

★ DES ★

Duke, the Chans, Glen, One-Armed, Big Les and I gather in a semi- circle, a few yards from the row of bookmakers, scratching our heads.

'Did everyone "get on"?' says Duke. We all nod. 'Then where the hell did he go?'

'Search me,' says Glen.

Duke cranes his neck and turns his head. 'It's like he just vanished into thin air.'

He takes out his cigarillos and lights one. Removing his mobile, he punches in Andy's number. No signal. 'He must have headed up to the hospitality box to join Rita. What do you reckon?'

Sammy glances at his watch. 'We'd better head up there, too. We don't want to miss the start.'

* * *

We jog to the grandstand foyer and pile into the elevator, alighting on the third floor. Duke consults the floor plan and points left. 'Manvers Road Star Racing Syndicate. Box twenty-four!' he says. We follow in his path and half way along the corridor, he stops in his tracks. 'In here.' We enter a spacious, well-lit room. A table runs down its middle, upon which lies several ice buckets, each one overflowing with cans of beer. Other than us, the place is empty.

'They're not here either,' says Glen.

'It's weird,' adds Big Les.

'They're in the gate. Stand by Wolverhampton,' announces Tommo.

We charge across the room to the balcony like a field of five-furlong sprinters, grabbing cans of beer en- route. The panoramic view over a floodlit Dunstall Park takes my breath away. I crack open my beer and take a swig as the gates fly open.

'And they're off! Racing to time at Dunstall Park.'

I close my eyes. Please God, *this* time.

Up in his commentary booth, Tommo describes the action. 'Manvers Road Star is best away.' My eyes shoot open at the mention of her name and I grip the balcony rail with both hands. Tommo's commentary rises in pitch as the action unfolds. 'Manvers Road Star and Seb Sanders grab the inside rail and lead Brave Emperor and Lunar Seas into the bend …'

I take a swig of beer. Beads of sweat appear on my forehead. 'It's the outsider in green and red silks Manvers Road Star, from Brave Emperor in the royal blue. Delquay, the favourite, is waited with out the back …' My heart starts thumping in my chest like a hammer. Beside me I hear Duke whispering a mantra softly under his breath, 'Go on, Star, go on Seb.'

I press my binoculars to my face. Seb Sanders and Star are full of running. 'The outsider of the field Manvers Road Star, skips two lengths clear!'

'Go on Seb!' roars Glen.

'Manvers Road Star straightens up for home!' proclaims Tommo.

'Go on Star!' I scream, adrenalin pumping through my veins.

With less than a furlong to go, Star is still in the clear, though the three market leaders are picking up and beginning to close the gap. We will her home like madmen, every hoof-print of the way.

'Go on Star!' shouts Duke.

'Go on Seb!' screams Glen.

'Go on girl!' An angelic image of Shirelle's face flashes into my mind. Three hundred yards from the finishing line, two hundred yards from the finishing line, Star is beginning to tie up – and though she has the measure of Brave Emperor and Lunar Ocean, Delquay is flying home. 'And here comes the favourite!' Tommo roars. I let out a gasp as Star bares down on the finishing line. She is startled seeing Delquay so late. Then, reminiscent of the 1990 Breeders Cup Sprint, she does a 'Dayjur' and sacrifices her small lead over Delquay by jumping the floodlit finishing line. Both horses flash past together. Tommo has the last word. 'That was close. I'll leave that one to the judge!'

'Photograph. Photograph, Wolverhampton', booms the senior steward.

My chest tightens. I gasp for air. I drop my binoculars. I clasp my heart with both hands. I can't breathe.

34

★ ANDY ★

A FEW MINUTES EARLIER

I run across the betting ring barking into my mobile phone. 'I'll wait for you outside the elevator in the grandstand foyer!' Seconds later I arrive. The elevator doors slide open to reveal a flustered looking Rita accompanied by a kindly tote lady. 'Deep breaths, Rita!' I say. I take her hand and we hurry as quickly as we can to the taxi rank outside the Holiday Inn.

'Where to mate?' asks the driver, slouched against his cab.

'Wolverhampton General – as fast as you can!'

* * *

I pace up and down outside Rita's room on the maternity ward. While my nostrils are twitching from the smell of disinfectant, a dark thought strikes me. *Why haven't I heard any newborn cries?*

The door handle slowly turns from the inside of Rita's room. A nurse emerges. I look at her expectantly for an update, but none is forthcoming. I rush past her into the room, fearing the worst. I see Rita, propped up in bed. Our eyes meet. Tears are rolling down her face as I reach her bedside. 'What is it?' I say. 'What's wrong, Rita?'

'My contractions.'

'What about them?'

'They just …'

'They just what?'

'They just stopped. It was a false alarm. I feel so stupid!'

I edge myself onto the bed. 'You're not stupid - if anyone around here should feel stupid, then it's me.'

'How do you mean?'

'Because, well - when I didn't hear any screams out there in the corridor, I was worried you might have …' My words tail off. I lie myself down beside her. Irrationally, I run my hand over her bump, just to be absolutely sure it's still there.

'Do you know if Star won?' she says. I just shrug my shoulders. 'Did you at least get your bet on?'

I remove my betting slip from my wallet and show her. She winces at the size of the stake. I sit up and try Duke's mobile in order to try to find out the result again. The reception is poor and I can't get a line.

'I don't suppose you feel like doing me a favour, do you?' she says, a little gingerly.

'Sure,' I say, replacing my phone in my pocket.

'You couldn't go and find me a fizzy drink? My sugar levels are in need of recharging.'

'Of course.'

'And when you return, promise me you'll get in a taxi back to the racecourse and enjoy the rest of the evening.'

'I was thinking of spending the night here?' I point at the sofa beside her bed.

'No – I insist. Besides, I have all these nurses to look after me. That's final. Drop by in the morning instead and fetch me on the way home.'

I shrug my shoulders and nod. 'Only if you're sure?'

She smiles. 'I'm sure.'

'Okay,' I reply. 'But first your drink.'

* * *

The vending machine on the maternity ward takes my pound coin without dispensing a drink.

I bang the side of it a couple of times but to no avail. I continue on my way through a labyrinth of corridors, until I find myself in the A & E waiting room. I spot another vending machine besides the reception counter. On my way over I stop in my tracks, when I notice a familiar face leaving the gents toilets.

'Les. Wait!'

Big Les turns around and walks over. 'Andy. What are you doing here?'

'I was going to ask you the same thing. Before I lose my mind, how did Star get on?'

'You don't know?'

'Of course I don't know! Why else would I be asking you?'

'She won, Andy! Or rather, what do you call it …'

'What? For fuck's sake Les, she either won or she didn't!'

'She dead-heated. That's the word. She dead-heated for first with the favourite!'

I punch my fist in to the air, as though celebrating scoring a late winner for The Pies. A look of concern sweeps across Big Les' face.

'What is it?' I say.

'No, it's just that if you didn't know Star won, I guess you haven't heard about Des?'

'Heard what?'

'Des collapsed just as the race finished. Out cold he was. We piled him in a taxi. I'm glad to say that he regained consciousness on the way here.'

For a moment I'm speechless. 'Bloody hell,' I mumble.

'It's alright, Andy. He's made a full recovery. I'm just on my way back to his ward now. Everyone is there.'

I regain my composure, before explaining my reason for being at the hospital.

'Poor Rita. Must have been a shock! How is she?'

'She's fine. Turns out it was a false alarm.'

Big Les goes quiet. 'As long as she's okay, like.'

I remember Rita's drink. I tap a short message to her into my mobile and press 'send.'

'Okay. Take me to Des.'

* * *

Within minutes, we're stood outside the door to Des' room. Opening it a few inches, Big Les whispers something inaudible to someone inside. There follow's some scuffling sounds from within before someone, I think it's Duke, calls out. 'Ready!' The door slowly opens. I enter and there they are - Sammy, Lee, Glen, Duke and One-Armed - cheering and applauding me, 'guard of honour style' along both sides of the room, with Des clapping the hardest, propped up against a mound of pillows.

'Nice one, Barney!' says Sammy Chan.

'You pulled it off, big fella!' says Duke, clapping me on the back.

'All I did was buy her, but thank you,' I say.

I make my way laughing and smiling to Des' bedside. 'You okay, mate?'

'I'm fine. It was nothing, just nerves, you know?'

'What does the doctor say?'

'I haven't seen one yet. But the nurses have checked me over and everything seems to be in order.'

'That's a relief. Big Les had me worried back there.'

'What a run from Star! It was, what's the word - electrifying. Everything we thought it would be. Magical!'

'I know. It's mad, isn't it?' I don't mention to Des that I haven't yet seen the race myself. Des goes on, 'and she still paid a handsome return, despite dead-heating!'

'Can you all please keep the noise down a bit!' Everyone turns their heads towards the doorway. Filling the door frame is a sturdily built nurse. 'Please spare a thought for Desmond's fellow patients, thank you!'

'Sorry, nurse,' says Duke.

'It's Sister Hodges,' she replies sternly. She adopts a friendlier tone at Des' bedside.

'Desmond, we'd like to keep you in for observation overnight.'

'I see,' says Des, struggling to hide his disappointment.

'Though you appear to be okay, we just want to run a few tests before we let you go.' With that, she heads towards the door, but not before turning to face everyone. 'Just to say, congratulations on your horse winning tonight. Desmond told me all about it!'

'Oh, cheers,' says Glen.

'Thanks, Sister,' adds Big Les.

As Sister Hodges heads off to continue her rounds, Des addresses us from his bed. 'Get yourselves back to the racecourse, boys - and don't forget to have a drink for me!'

'Are you sure, mate?' says Glen.

'There isn't much point to you all hanging around here – and if you get a move on, you'll make it back in time for the "lucky last." Not sure how Seb's second ride went, but I can't be the only one here who has a few quid running onto his last ride?' As everyone starts checking their multiple bets, Des calls me over. 'Can you do me a favour, Andy?'

'Sure. What is it?'

'Will you collect my winnings for me?'

'Of course.' Des hands me a roll of tote slips and bookmakers' cards. 'And while you're at it, give me the slips you put on it town earlier today,' I add.

'Good thinking,' says Des.

'We'll pick you up in the morning, after we've collected our money in town. That way, we can head back direct to Nottingham from here.'

'Okay, cool – and thanks.'

'Just so you know, you're not the only one from our group being kept in for observation.'

'How do you mean?'

I briefly fill Des in on my adventure with Rita earlier in the evening. We say our farewells from the doorway. A chorus of farewells fill the room. 'See you tomorrow, mate!'

Des waves back from his bed. 'Will do. And have fun!'

* * *

I appear in Rita's doorway, holding up two cans of drink.

'There you are,' she says as I enter. 'I was thinking I might need to send out a search party!'

'Rita, I'll explain,' I say approaching the bed. 'But first, guess what?'

Rita holds her mouth up to her face. 'She didn't go and win, did she?'

'She dead-heated for first, which amounts to the same thing!'

'Come here!!' she says. I hop up onto the bed and she hugs me tightly.

'Sprite or Pepsi?' I say.

'Sprite, please.'

Rita smiles as I reach inside my coat and produce a can of lager that Glen gave me in Des' room.

'Cheers!'

'Cheers!', says Rita. We pull our can tops simultaneously. They both explode, showering us in lemonade and lager. We both lay there laughing hysterically. Eventually, I dampen a towel in the hand basin and we take it in turns to wipe our faces. I fill Rita in on how I ran into Big Les in A & E and all about Des.

'Blimey. It's been quite an evening,' she says.

'Tell me about it! Okay, the boys will be waiting for me in the foyer. Promise to call me if your contractions start again?'

'What will you be able to do about it, if they do?' she laughs.

'Then I'll come back, fast as. Otherwise, I'll drop by in the van tomorrow to collect you and Des before we head home.'

'Alright. Have fun – and Andy?'

'Yeah?'

'Congratulations. About Star, I mean. You did it.'

35

★ ANDY ★

By the time we arrive back at Dunstall Park the sun has set, leaving a soft pink and green stain across the Black Country night sky. The place is buzzing, people laughing, shouting, betting and drinking – animated shadows darting in and out of pools of yellowish light and bluey-black shadow. We stand in a semi-circle on the edge of the parade ring. 'How about we all go and collect our winnings?' I say. 'Then we can drop by the hotel and lock them in our room safes?'

'Good thinking,' says Duke.

'Sounds like a plan, adds Big Les.

* * *

I approach the 'Bull Dog' bookie on pitch number one. He scowls when he sees me and after paying me out, I hear him cursing me under his breath as I walk away. 'Nice doing business with you too,' I say, smiling. I collect Des' winnings a bit further along the rails. Afterwards I visit one of the tote counters inside the grandstand building where, shrewdie that he is, his combination tricast ticket alone pays a four figure sum.

* * *

With our winnings safely stashed away behind lock and key, we reconvene in the hotel foyer.

'I wonder if we can find Ray and Ellie?' I say. 'I tried ringing earlier but the signal here is terrible.'

'Let's hope they've not already set off home,' says Big Les.

'Hang on. I've got an idea,' I say. 'C'mon, follow me.'

I lead everyone to the entrance to the weighing room, where I approach a racecourse official.

'Hello. We're all members of the Manvers Road Star Racing Syndicate.'

'Okay, Sir. How can I help you?'

'I wondered if you could you arrange for a message to be broadcast over the tannoy?'

'I'll see what I can do.' He disappears inside. A moment later he returns and handing me a pad and pen, asks me to jot down my message. Moments later, we beam proudly as the words I wrote ring out over the racecourse tannoy.

'Would the trainer Ray Baldwin and his Head Lass Ellie McGovern, please report to the weighing room where members of the Manvers Road Racing Syndicate are waiting for you. That's a message for Ray Baldwin, the trainer of Manvers Road Star and Head Lass Ellie Mc Govern, please come immediately to the weighing room. Thank you.'

* * *

Within minutes, Ray and Ellie appear. Before they have the chance to quiz me about our 'no show' in the winner's enclosure, I throw myself at them. 'You bloody geniuses!' I just have time to kiss them both on the cheek, before they're mobbed by the others. To passers-by, we probably resemble some kind of deliriously happy rugby scrum, a noisy mass rotating as one in the shadow of the weighing room building.

'So, what happened to you all, earlier?' says Ray. I bring them up to speed on the dramas involving Des and Rita. 'Blimey,' he says. 'Well, I hope you all had a proper bet? 'I know I did!' He laughs and everyone joins in.

Ellie turns to me and hands me a thin square white envelope. 'Before I forget, this is for you.' I open it. Inside is a DVD disk. 'What's on it?'

'A recording of Star's race, of course,' she says.

'Oh, nice one!'

'When none of you showed up in the winner's circle, Ray asked me to stand in as "owner's representative". The DVD was given to me by Dunstall Park's head of marketing – along with an engraved glass decanter. That's in the horsebox for safe keeping.'

'Thanks for stepping in for us.' I turn to Ray. 'Any chance of us seeing Star before you head back to Edwinstowe?'

'Of course,' he says. 'Ellie and I were just on our way to the loading bay when we received your message. C'mon – it's this way.'

* * *

We wait in the floodlit loading bay area. A silver horse-transport vehicle pulls over. *Ray Baldwin Racing* is emblazoned along its side in a stylish maroon font. Ray jumps out of the driver's compartment and opens up the back. As the others head over to join him, we hear the clip-clop of hooves on tarmac behind us. I turn around and there's the apple of my eye, being led towards us by a beaming Ellie. I stand in front of her in complete awe. I tilt my head in towards her. Turning her head into profile, she looks directly at me through her good eye. Moving her head closer, I stroke her white blaze and gently hold her head in my hands. Then something magical happens. She starts nuzzling me.

'Thank you, Star,' I whisper.

Ellie, who has been watching our exchange, says, 'Back in a second – stay here.'

I nod. Ellie heads off. A moment later she reappears at my side.

'Your prize,' she says, handing me the glass decanter.

'Thank you!' I hold it in my hands and study it. 'I wondered if we'd get just half a decanter, given that we dead-heated.'

Ellie laughs. 'That's what the owner of Delquay said!' I hold the decanter proudly in my hands. 'I have something for you, too.' Duke, Sammy, Lee and the others gather around as I hand her an envelope.

'Me and the lads wanted you to have this,' I say.

Ellie opens the envelope. Inside is a wad of ten-and twenty-pound notes.

'Andy, boys ... 'she says.

'Star would never have run like she did tonight without your expert care and attention - simple as.'

'I don't know what to say?' she says.

'Nothing *to* say,' Sammy says, smiling.

Ellie slips the envelope into her jeans pocket. 'Thank you.'

With that, she turns and leads Star up a ramp and into the horsebox. Ray comes over. 'Let's talk early next week, Andy.

I reckon we should run her again soon - strike while the iron is hot, you know?' I nod and we shake hands. Turning to address everyone, he says, 'have a great night, boys!'

His words are received with a chorus of wild cheers. Ray bolts up the back of the horsebox and heads to the drivers compartment with Ellie in tow. The seven of us stand there and watch as they pull out of the loading bay – and with a toot of the horn, Ray, Ellie and Star disappear out of the racecourse gates into the Black Country night.

* * *

For a while, we just stand there in the floodlit loading bay in contented silence. It's a moment I will never forget, though Rita and Des are conspicuous in their absence.

'Dun, dud-un! Dun, dud-un! Dun, dud-un! Dun, dud-un, dun …' A sudden burst of music blasts over the racecourse PA. Glen starts nodding his head in time to it. 'I recognise this song – what's it called?'

Duke starts nodding his head in time to it too. 'I know – "It's Not Unusual" by Tom Jones.'

'The Tom Jones tribute gig! ' blurts Sammy.

'Oh yeah!' I say.

'It's time we celebrated Star's win …' adds Big Les.

Sammy fixes his eyes on me. 'All right everyone. Let's grab him!'

I didn't stand a chance. The six of them charge at me and before I can muster any resistance, I'm hoisted up on to Duke's shoulders. Somehow, in the ensuing melee, I manage to keep hold of the glass decanter and carried along in the spirit of the moment, thrust it 'Bobby Moore style' above my head like it was the Jules Rimet trophy, as they carry me laughing and singing towards the music.

* * *

At just after one o' clock in the morning, to the strains of 'Delilah', we stumble out of the hall behind the grandstand and stagger the short distance to our hotel. Approaching the entrance, I sidle up to Sammy Chan. 'For a moment, I thought you'd pulled that tall brunette you were dancing with.' Everyone whistles and jeers.

'Me too,' says Sammy, 'till her body builder boyfriend walked over!'

* * *

Fumbling in my pocket for the key card to my room, I find the DVD disk. Once inside my room, I make a beeline for the TV. Removing the disk carefully from its sleeve, I switch on the DVD player and slot it the into the tray. With a quiet swish sound, it closes. Just as I'm about to press 'play', an idea strikes me: *Why not ring everyone using the room-to-room telecom, so we can watch it together?*

I look out Duke's room number and pick up the phone – but just as I'm about to dial, I think again. With the exception of Rita, the only person who is yet to have seen Star's moment of glory is *me.* I put down the receiver and noticing the fridge, fumble inside the mini bar. I find a tin of cashew nuts, a can of lager and to my delight, a miniature Irish whiskey. I remove all three, make myself comfortable on the bed, take a swig of whiskey, crack open the beer and nibbling on the cashew nuts, pick up the remote control and press 'play.'

36

★ ANDY ★

Fuelled by several cups of strong coffee and a hearty breakfast, we check out of the Holiday Inn and set off in the transit van for Wolverhampton town centre. On the way, we boisterously re-live the highlights of Star's moment of glory the previous evening. I park in the Manders Shopping Centre car park as I did yesterday, timing our arrival just as the town's betting shops open their doors for trade. We gather in a group outside the car park. It's a bright sunny morning. 'All right, so how's this for a plan: after collecting our winnings, we'll head straight to Wolverhampton General. Then after collecting Rita and Des, we'll drive back to Nottingham and continue our celebrations at the King Billy. What do you say?' Everyone cheers. 'Let's meet back here when we're all done. Bear with me, as I'm collecting Des' money too.'

* * *

After collecting my and Rita's winnings, I set about visiting the shops in Des and One-Armed section. On my way to the counter inside the last one, a branch of Coral, nature calls and I head into the gents. On my way to the urinals, I pass an open toilet cubicle, the larger kind reserved for wheelchair users. And there, stood inside, is One-Armed Bruce. I watch him busily feeding several thick wads of bank notes into the lining of his coat. It is immediately obvious to me that he had far more on Star than the amount we all agreed to.

'All right, Bruce?'

He turns around. 'Andy?' He looks at me with an anxious smile.

'Bloody hell. How much did *you* have on?'

Though I'd rumbled him, Bruce clearly believed that the best form of defence was attack. 'Not as much as I'd wanted to - but I had to at least partly compensate myself for the good turn I did you last year.'

'What are you talking about?'

'Who do you think helped your dad place that bet? The one that made you so rich?'

It felt like such a long time ago, now - that Saturday in September last year; the afternoon dad and I went fishing up at Kingfisher Lakes, while Frankie Dettori rode himself into the history books at Ascot. And though I hadn't been aware that Bruce had helped dad fill out his betting slip, I can't help thinking that he not been around to do so, Glen would have helped dad at the counter. But Bruce isn't finished with me yet.

'This has all been one big ego trip for you, hasn't it?'

'How do you mean?'

'Buying Star. Showing off in front of your mates.'

'What?' I say. 'I bought Star for all of us! Des had just come out of hospital after a check-up on his heart and I knew that Lee and Sammy had their worries about the Flying Dragon. You also made it very clear how tired you'd become of your bloody security job! I thought involving you with Star might cheer you up! Don't blame me if you haven't tried to do something about changing your situation!'

His eyes darken - and picking up the rest of his winnings from the bag at his feet, he pushes past me, almost knocking me over. 'You don't know the half of it, Andy. Fuck this, I'll make my own way back to Nottingham!'

* * *

There isn't the time for me to try to process what just happened. I force it into the back of my mind and after collecting the last of Des' winnings, return to meet the others. I'm the last to arrive.

'All good, Andy?' says Duke.

'Yeah. All good.'

'Any one seen One-Armed?' says Big Les.

I improvise. 'When I was fetching Des' winnings, I met him in Coral's. His wife Collette rang. He's getting the train to Nottingham direct. Some family situation, nothing serious.'

Everyone is in such high spirits they seem to buy my explanation.

* * *

Within twenty minutes, I pull the van into Wolverhampton General Hospital car park. As we approach the entrance, Duke has a suggestion.

'How about us lot go and fetch Des, while you fetch Rita?'

'Sure,' I say.

Inside we split up. I arrive at the reception desk on the maternity ward. Sister Adams greets me with a friendly smile.

'Good morning, Sister. How is our patient?' I say.

'She's fine, Mr Cooper. No new episodes – or twins waiting to make your acquaintance!'

'Oh, good,' I say, suppressing a burst of nervous laughter.

She leads me onto the ward and arriving outside Rita's room, knocks on the door.

'Rita, I have a certain someone here for you?'

Rita opens the door and smiles. 'Hi, Andy,' she says. We hug in the doorway.

'Hi gorgeous,' I say.

She's all dressed and ready to go. She turns to Sister Adams. 'Thank you. You've been so kind to me.'

'My pleasure, Rita. And best of luck with when your baby does arrive. I don't think it will be a long wait, from what I've seen and heard.'

'All set?' I say.

'All set,' says Rita.

And with that, we leave the maternity ward arm in arm.

* * *

As we arrive in the hospital foyer, my mobile phone starts ringing. I remove it from my jacket pocket and answer. It's Duke.

'All right, Duke?' There follows a strange silence from the other end of the line. 'Duke? Are you there?'

'Yeah. Sorry. Are you in the hospital foyer?'

I stop in my tracks. 'We just got here. Is everything okay?' Another silence follows. 'Duke?'

'Find somewhere to sit down. There's been a – something's happened.'

37

★ MARSHA ★

NINE HOURS EARLIER

I'm woken in the dead of night by the sound of my bedside telephone. I switch on the lamp beside my bed, dazed and bleary eyed. I check the time. One twenty-three. Rubbing sleep from my eyes I pick up the handset.

'Marsha James?'

'Yes. Who's this?'

'This is Wolverhampton General Hospital.'

'Okay …'

'My name is Sister Hodges. I'm ringing about your father, Desmond?'

I sit upright in bed. 'What's happened?'

'Is it possible for you to come in, Marsha?'

'Yes, I'm just fifteen minutes away. Why?'

'Your dad will be undergoing some quite serious surgery, about an hour from now.'

My mouth feels dry and my heart starts racing. 'What's happened?'

'He was admitted last night, after he feinted at Dunstall Park Racecourse. '

'What?'

'His friends brought him in. He regained consciousness on the way. We gave him a general check over and everything seemed okay, until …'

'Until what?'

'Until a couple of hours ago, when he … took a turn for the worse.'

I shoot out of bed and head to Kyle's room. I knock on the door and enter. He's up, playing a computer game. He turns to face me. I fight to hold back my tears.

'Kyle, it's your grandpa.'

* * *

Sister Hodges meets us at reception and leads us to dad. She briefs us before entering.

'His test results show there were no signs of any heart trouble. But when we got his scan results, we discovered your dad has an embolism. That's what caused him to feint last night.'

I squeeze Kyle's hand. 'It's lodged itself in an artery close to his lungs. He's receiving morphine to make him more comfortable. He's drowsy but conscious. I thought you might like to sit with him?'

'Thank you,' I say.

'I'll give you some privacy,' says Sister Hodges, turning towards the door. 'Press the button by the bed if you need me.'

* * *

Kyle and I pick up two chairs and sit ourselves down beside dad's bed. He's lying on his back, breathing deeply. I take his hand. After a short while his eyelids flicker. Slowly he opens his eyes. He turns to face me. 'Marsha?'

'Hello, Dad.' His voice is weak, but he manages a faint smile. 'Kyle is here, too,' I say.

I place my other hand in Kyle's. Kyle squeezes it tightly. Dad looks at Kyle and smiles.

'Hello Kyle,' says Dad.

'Hello Grandpa.'

Dad starts breathing very deliberately - hard, deep breathes. Summoning his strength, he says, 'You'll never guess what?'

'What?'

'She won! Star.'

'That's brilliant,' says Kyle.

'Nice one, Dad.' I say.

He closes his eyes. I hear Kyle sniff. I turn to look at him and see him wipe the tears from his face self-consciously. I squeeze his hand tighter. A minute or two pass, before dad regains consciousness. Through tired eyes he turns and looks at me. 'Marsha?' I move my chair as close to the side of the bed as is possible. 'If I … well - in case ...' Slowly but surely my tears begin to fall. 'I have two really important things to tell you.'

'Okay.'

'Are you listening carefully?'

I squeeze his hand gently. 'I am.'

'You know that photo album? The one we like looking through from time to time?' I nod. 'Well, there's another one I keep in that draw, underneath it. It has a blue cover.' Dad takes a breather, rests and then continues. 'I always meant to find the time to show it to you but the right moment never seemed to come along.' He goes quiet for a moment before continuing. 'I want you and Kyle to take a look at it. Go through it together. Do you promise you'll do that?'

'Of course. I promise.'

He smiles. 'Good. And I want you to show it to Andy too.'

'To Andy? Alright. Of course.'

Dad looks momentarily satisfied, calm. 'Now, where's that grandson of mine?' he says, raising a faint smile. Kyle moves closer to dad's bedside. 'Come here,' says dad. Kyle puts his arms around dad and holds him tightly. Summoning his strength, dad looks Kyle in the eyes. 'I hope you know just how proud I am of you? Working at Ray's?'

Kyle wipes his blotchy eyes with the back of his hand and sits back in his chair. Here we sit, helpless, watching dad fade away.

'Marsha,' he whispers.

'Yes, dad?'

'I'm cold.'

A pile of blankets lye neatly stacked at the end of the bed. Kyle and I get up and fetch one each and carefully wrap them around his small body, tucking the blankets in gently at his sides. Dad drifts away again and for a moment, I think he's gone. Briefly, he returns.

'The Autumn,' he whispers.

'What's that, Dad?'

'The best time of the year to see Bridgetown,' he says, giving my hand a gentle squeeze. I grip his hand tightly. He does the same, but slowly I feel his grip weaken - and just a few seconds pass, before his hand releases mine.

38

★ ANDY ★

Rita and I sit down beside one another on a row of outpatient benches. To her left sits a man wrapped from head to toe in bandage and to my right, a woman wearing an elaborate head brace.

'Andy, Rita …' We turn around simultaneously. It's Duke. His face is ashen grey. I make to stand, but he gestures to me to remain seated. He sinks into the seat opposite.

'What is it?' I say.

Duke looks down at his feet and fidgets with the fingers on his large hands.

'Duke?' says Rita.

He looks up. 'There's no easy way of saying this, so I'm …' His words tail off. He starts over. 'It's Des. He's - Des has passed away.'

Bang. Rita lets out a cry. I slump forward in my seat. In my mind's eye, a red star falls from our green racing silks. Rita is distraught. I put my arms around her.

'According to the duty nurse, he died at just after two o'clock this morning. His daughter Marsha and Kyle were at his side.'

'It's too awful!' cries Rita through her tears.

I make to say something, but no words come. 'What was the cause of death?' I mumble.

'I forgot to ask, I … I couldn't stand being in that room a moment longer.'

Just as I'm about to ask where the others have got to, I look up – and there stood before me are Big Les, Glen, Sammy and Lee. Big Les looks as white as a ghost. Glen's eyes are a milky red. I get to my feet and embrace each of them in turn. I return to Rita's side. She looks up at me. Her eyes are raw red and sore looking. 'Can we just get out of here?' she says. 'I just want to get home to Sneinton.' And with that, we file out of the hospital in silence.

As I unlock the van door, Duke approaches me. 'Sister Adams asked me to give you this.' Duke hands me an envelope.

'What is it?'

'I don't know. She just asked me to make sure that I handed it to you in person.'

* * *

After parting in silence from the others on Manvers Road, Rita and I arrive back at the flat. I dump our winnings in a bag in the hallway. Des' winnings, just north of fourteen grand, I leave on the living room table. I fetch a beer from the kitchen and take out the envelope Duke gave me. While Rita unpacks her overnight case in silence, I sit down on the sofa and read it.

Andy, I am too weak and tired to write this note myself. Thankfully, Sister Adams offered to write it for me. She has promised to make sure that it gets to you, in the event that I don't, well, pull through.

I know that I can count on you getting the money I won to my daughter, Marsha. I have included her telephone number below. Perhaps you can call her and arrange to meet up? When you give it to her, you are to tell her that it's the money for Barbados. That's really important. She'll understand what you mean. Her number is 0121-435 712.

Your friend, Des.

Rita comes over. I show her the note and she picks it up and reads it. I look at the telephone, consumed with anxiety. 'What do I say to her?'

Rita detects my edginess. 'Offer your condolences and then tell her what a great friend Des was to you. Then tell her that you have her dad's winnings here.' A silence falls over us.

'Andy. What is it?'

'I'm scared …'

'What are you scared of?'

'Scared she'll resent me. For Des dying.'

Rita places her hand on my shoulder. 'Andy, you …'

'If I hadn't involved Des with Star, he'd still have been alive today.'

Rita looks at me. 'You don't know that …'

'No. But despite knowing that he had issues with his heart, it didn't stop me from making him a part-owner in a racehorse! If anything was going to set off his dodgy ticker, it would have been that!'

'Andy -'

'She'll resent me - just like dad resented me when mum died while we were down at Wembley last year!' I break down.

Rita sits down beside me. 'This situation isn't the same. It's just triggering the feelings you had about how your dad treated you at the time.'

For a while we just sit there in silence. 'I just can't believe he's dead,' I say. 'Since losing dad, Des had felt like a ....'

Rita takes my face in her hands. 'I know.'

'I … I'm just going to miss him so much.' Rita kisses me. I reach for my beer and quickly finish it. 'I will ring Marsha, but not this minute.' Rita looks at me. 'I just need to clear my head first – go for a walk, get some fresh air.'

Rita nods. 'Of course.' She holds her tummy. 'While you are out, I think I might lay down for a while.'

I lift myself out of my seat and put my arms around her. 'Good idea,' I say.

* * *

I head past Sanjay's and before long, find myself walking in the direction of the cemetery. When I get there, I touch the top of mum and dad's gravestones and then sit down on my bench, a storm raging in my head. I light a cigarette and try to make sense of the past few days: Rita's 'false alarm', the 'high' of Star winning and then Des passing away, all within the space of a few hours. The cemetery doesn't feel like a sanctuary today, as there is no peace of mind to be salvaged from what has happened – and twenty minutes after arriving I make my way home none the wiser, to make a phone call I don't want to make.

* * *

Back at the flat, the living room is empty. I walk to the bedroom door and quietly open it. Rita is lying on the bed on her side, sleeping soundly. I close the door carefully and pour myself a large whiskey in the living room. I take a swig, pick up the telephone, sit down on the sofa and slowly dial Marsha's number.

39

★ MARSHA ★

I turn the final page of the photo album and gently close it. I lean back into the sofa, my head spinning. Sat beside me is Kyle. We look at one another at exactly the same moment.

'Well, would you believe it?' I say.

'So, Grandpa was –'

The sound of the telephone ringing cuts him short. I pick up.

'Hello, Marsha speaking.'

'Hello. Er, my name is Andy. I was a friend of your dad's.'

'Oh, hello.'

'I … I'm so sorry for your loss.'

'Thank you.'

'Your dad and I owned a racehorse together with some other friends?'

'Andy, that's right - Dad spoke a lot about you. And thank you, incidentally.'

'For what?'

'For helping, you know. Kyle.'

'I can't take any credit there, but thanks all the same.' A short silence follows. 'How *is* Kyle?'

'Oh, you know. Sad, but coping. Like me.'

'Your dad, he - let's just say, I considered him a true friend.'

I smile down the telephone. 'That's good to know.'

'Which makes this, well … extra difficult, talking to you.'

'Why?'

The line goes quiet. Kyle picks up the photo album from the glass table. As he opens it, some loose clippings and papers fall out from the back of the album onto the carpet. He stoops down under the glass table, gathers them together and replaces them.

'Are you still there? Why does this seem difficult, talking with me?'

'Well, given that I knew your dad had trouble with his heart.'

I consider his words carefully. 'I'm not sure what they told you at the hospital, but dad didn't die from a heart condition.'

'He didn't?'

'No. They discovered he had an embolism.'

'Oh.'

'I'm just glad that Kyle and I made it to the hospital in time, you know, before he –'. My eyes well up. 'Sorry, I …'

'Don't be,' Andy says.

I re-compose myself, gather my thoughts. I look at the photo album in Kyle's hands.

'Can we meet up? I have something here that dad wanted me to show you.'

'Of course. I was going to ask you the same thing. I have something of your dad's to give you too.'

'Okay.' I think for a moment. 'How would the day after tomorrow suit?'

'Tuesday afternoon would be fine. You live in Birmingham, right?'

'Yes.'

'I'll get a train down.'

'Okay. Ring me when you know what time you'll get in to New Street Station.'

'All right, I'll do that, and …'

'Yes?'

'Thank you - you know – for explaining …'

40

★ ANDY ★

At just after eleven on a sunny Autumn morning, the Nottingham to Birmingham train pulls into platform five at New Street Station. I shuffle through the carriage to the middle doors, carrying a holdall containing over fourteen grand in cash. I show my ticket at the barrier and enter the station concourse. I notice a petite West Indian woman in her late thirties. She looks at me with an uncertain smile. She is dressed casual smart, an orange beret capping her medium length frizzy hair. She holds a tote bag in her left hand, out of which pokes the top of a blue book.

'Andy?' she says as I approach.

'Marsha?' I smile. We shake hands and then embrace a little awkwardly.

'Nice to meet you - even if the circumstances could have been happier,' I say.

'Yes - I still can't believe that he's gone. It's all so weird. A short silence follows. 'Er, are you hungry?'

'I will be, soon.'

'I know an Italian place, not far from here?' she says.

* * *

We take a right turn outside the station and make our way slowly along a canal side pathway. It's lined with small boutiques and cafes.

'I'll be up this way again tomorrow, seeing Kyle off,' she says.

'Right.'

'It's good he'll have the distraction of the stable to take his mind off things. Ellie is going to collect him at Nottingham station and drive him up there tomorrow afternoon.'

'Kyle seems a real natural around horses, Marsha.'

She stops outside a smart restaurant with a white facade called Antonio's and smiles. 'Perhaps that isn't so strange,' she says a little cryptically.

'How do you mean?'

'I'll get to get to that in time, I promise.'

* * *

Antonio's is only about one third full, but is quickly filling up with lunchtime custom. A waiter greets us and shows us to a window side table where we order a bottle of wine. He returns, pours two glasses and leaves a decanter of water.

'To your dad,' I say, holding up my glass.

'Yes – to Dad.' We clink glasses. 'You know, Kyle and I almost lost him once before, a few years back - figuratively speaking, that is.'

'How do you mean?'

'In 1991, after my mum died. Naturally, we were all devastated. Her death was so sudden. I think I under-estimated the impact her passing away would have on dad. I was married at the time and Kyle had just turned nine. While mum was alive, he'd always been such an active dad – great with Kyle, sociable with Del, Kyle's dad, that is. But then after mum died, he changed.'

'Changed in what way?'

'He withdrew into himself.' Marsha takes a sip of wine. 'Looking back, I think it was because mum had been his only living connection to Barbados.' I nod and take a sip of wine. 'How long had you been friends?'

'Just over two years. I met him at my local bookies. Your dad was one of a group of people who have since become firm friends. They were a great support to me after I lost my parents – my mum in 1995 and then dad last year.'

'I'm so sorry,' she says.

I take a sip of wine. 'Thank you. Without your dad and the others, I sometimes wonder what would have become of me. Then last October, I won a lot of money. It gave me the chance to show them my gratitude, which is why I bought us Star. Her full name is Manvers Road Star. We named her after the betting shop where we all became friends, you see.'

Marsha smiles. 'I never knew that.' She takes a sip of wine and glances out of the window.

'So, you and Des lost touch for a while?' I say.

'Yes. There was a lot going on in all our lives following mum's passing. My marriage was in trouble and Kyle started having problems. Dad did his best to be supportive during the break- up of my marriage but whenever we met up, it was like there was this big absence that we both felt. Mum. After Del and I divorced, dad and I slowly drifted apart.' A short silence falls over the table. I offer Marsha a refill and she accepts. Our waiter comes over and takes our orders. Marsha continues. 'Then earlier this year, completely out of the blue, dad rings me. We'd barely had contact in six years.'

'I see.'

'He invited Kyle and I up to Nottingham. Kyle was at his dad's that week, so I went alone. We had such a nice evening. He made me my favourite Bajan dish.' I nod and smile. 'He was just like his old self again - affectionate, engaging, funny. We didn't once dwell upon why we'd lost touch. That may sound odd, but it just felt so nice, having him back. Besides, I'd been equally compliant in letting things slip as he'd been.'

I take a sip of wine and nod.

'That evening, I discovered the reason for the change in him.'

'And what was that?'

Marsha pauses as our waiter arrives with our food. After he leaves, she smiles broadly and looks me in the eyes. 'Manvers Road Star.'

'Star?'

'Yes – Star.'

'Sorry, you've lost me.'

Marsha's eyes fill up. 'By involving dad with Star, you brought him back into our lives.' Now it's my turn to become dewy eyed. Marsha goes on. 'The evening he cooked for me he left out the certificate you gave him. The one showing him as a one-eighth owner in Star. He was so proud. Star coming into his life enabled him to finally move on after losing mum. Involvement with your syndicate gave him something to look forward to, rather than spend his days pining for mum. Star brought purpose back into his life, which led to him reaching out to me and re-entering my and Kyle's lives.' I well up. Marsha reaches for my hand between our empty plates. I let her take it. She looks me in the eyes and smiles. 'So, thank you.'

'I had absolutely no idea', I say, wiping away a tear.

She gently withdraws her hand from mine and looks

down at the side of the table. Moving our dinner plates to one side, she removes the photo album from her bag. She places it between us. 'And that's not all,' she says.

'How do you mean?'

By involving dad with Star, you enabled him to reconnect with his past.

41

★ ANDY ★

I look at the book laid out before me. 'What's this?'

'A photo album,' says Marsha. 'Or rather, a cross between a photo album and a scrap book.'

She takes a sip of wine. 'Dad kept two photo albums in a draw in the living room at home. One with a red cover and then this one. The red one I've been familiar with for as long as I can remember. It contains photographs of mum and dad when they began courting back in Barbados and photographs of their wedding day. There are also photographs of me when I was little after they had moved to England, as well as some pictures dad took in Costa Brava of our first holiday abroad.' She hesitates briefly before continuing. 'But *this* album.' She taps the blue cover with the index finger of her right hand, 'I didn't know existed until he told me about it, the night he died.'

I'm intrigued.

'Dad made it very clear to me that I show it to you, which is why I've brought it along today.'

Our waiter arrives and takes our plates. 'Would you like

some desserts?' he says. Marsha looks at me. 'I'm good, thanks,' I say. 'But perhaps another bottle of wine?'

'Good idea,' says Marsha. I've a feeling you're going to need it.' Then she raises herself out of her chair, rounds the table and sits down beside me.

* * *

She opens the cover. It's a standard size photo album, eleven by fourteen-inches in size. I look at the photograph on the facing page. It's a black and white full-length portrait. Looking out from the page is a lean, Afro-Caribbean male in his mid-twenties. He's smiling proudly, dressed in quartered jockey silks and cap, riding britches and leather boots. He holds a riding whip in his left hand. My eyes hone in on the jockey's face. I study his features and slowly look at Marsha. Our wine arrives and she tops up our glasses in silence. I look at the photograph a second time and take a mouthful. When I look up, Marsha's gaze is fixed on me.

'Is this who I *think* it is?' I say.

She smiles and takes a sip of wine. 'Read the caption at the bottom of the photograph, if you're in any doubt.'

My eyes dart to the bottom of the photograph, where I read the following words. *'Me in the parade ring, ahead of my first professional ride. Garrison Savannah Racecourse, 1954.'*

'Bloody hell …'

'Hard to get your head around, isn't it?' she says.

'Des was a jockey?'

Marsha smiles at me and nods. 'Strictly speaking, he was an apprentice jockey.' She turns the page and points at the following double spread. 'But going by these newspaper cuttings, he was clearly a promising one. Marsha looks with interest as I slowly turn the pages - a mixture of original photographs and press cuttings from the sports pages of the Barbados Advocate. The newspaper print has turned a sepia yellow with age. I stop and look at a faded colour photograph of him with a wreath of flowers around his neck, stood on the winner's podium – and another one of a triumphant looking Des being lead in to the winner's enclosure, dothing his cap, right arm raised, surrounded by well-wishers, beaming proudly.

'May I?' says Marsha.

'Sure.'

Marsha turns the pages carefully and finds the item she was searching for. 'Read this.'

She points to a newspaper headline. I read it out loud. 'Desmond James: one victory away from being crowned the 1955 Champion Apprentice Jockey of Barbados.' I read the first paragraph on the story. 'If twenty-four- year- old Desmond James rides one more winner this coming Saturday at Garrison Savannah, he will be crowned champion apprentice jockey. James is expected to have a full book of rides from his supporters among the training ranks.' Accompanying the article is a photograph of Des riding a finish in full flight. I turn to the next page. It's blank. I turn the next one and the one after that. Both pages are blank. The newspaper cutting is the album's final entry. I look at Marsha.

'So, did he do it? Become champion?'

Marsha looks at me and sucks her teeth. 'No, he didn't. Sadly, the meeting was abandoned.'

'No! How come?'

'On Wednesday 21st September, 1955, the day after that article was published, Barbados was hit by the worst natural disaster in the country's history. A tropical cyclone named Hurricane Janet. By the time the weekend arrived, the racecourse had been completely devastated. A state of national emergency was declared. Eighty- nine people lost their lives, including my grandpa on dad's side.'

'That's terrible.'

'It took years for the country to recover. Fairly early on, mum and dad took the decision to emigrate, taking offers of jobs here in England as a means of survival.' I sit in stunned silence.

Marsha goes on. 'While there were many bigger tragedies among dad's countrymen and women caused by Hurricane Janet, it robbed him of the chance to be crowned the best young jockey on the island.' I sit there, speechless. Marsha continues. 'The fixture list that year was never completed. As yet, I've been unable to find out when exactly when racing resumed. All I do know though for sure is that by the time it did, mum and dad had started their lives over in Nottingham.' Another brief silence falls over the table. Eventually Marsha says, 'I understand, this is a lot to take in.'

I pour the last of the wine into our glasses. 'Yes, it is.'

Marsha gazes out of the window again. 'I'll never know if dad ever tried to make it here as a jockey. Circumstances almost certainly conspired against him; the immediate need to support himself and mum. Perhaps he simply decided to leave that chapter of his life behind him?' She takes a sip of wine and looks at me. 'One thing really warms my heart, though.'

'What's that?'

'How proud dad must have felt when he discovered Kyle had inherited his affinity with horses?'

I nod. 'That's a great thought to take from all of this.'

Marsha excuses herself to visit the toilets. When she returns, she sits down in her original place opposite me.

'Thank you for sharing this with me.'

Marsha smiles. 'You're welcome.'

A brief silence falls over our table. It's me who breaks it.

'I also have something of your dad's with me – something he asked me to deliver to you in person, in a note that his nurse wrote to me on his behalf.' I pick up the holdall beside my chair and place it on the table between us. 'The money he won on Star.' Marsha gives me a surprised look. 'Did he mention it to you?'

'No. Only that Star won.'

'Well,' I say, nudging the holdall a little closer towards her. 'The money in this holdall now belongs to you.' Marsha stares at it blankly. 'Would you like to know how much is in there?' I add.

'Sure - I mean, it would save us the time of getting it all out and counting it!' Marsha laughs nervously.

'Fourteen thousand, seven hundred and twenty-seven pounds'.

Marsha gasps. *'How much?'*

She appears genuinely shocked. I go on. 'And in the note, he said that I was to tell you that it's the "Barbados money". He said you would understand what he meant.'

'Oh Dad,' she whispers, just as a tear trickles down her cheek.

* * *

I'm not used to drinking a bottle of wine at lunchtime; and going by her unsteady stride, neither is Marsha. As we wander back towards New Street Station along the side of the canal, she links her arm in mine. Reaching the station entrance, we place ourselves in the taxi queue. 'The funeral is next Sunday,' she says. 'It's at two thirty in the afternoon, at the church dad used to go to in St Anns.' I nod. 'Kyle and I will drive up to Nottingham the day before. We thought we'd stay the night at dad's place. I've taken a week's bereavement leave, you know, to sort through dad's stuff and clean the house.'

'Okay,' I say.

'I was thinking,' she continues. 'The evening before the funeral, I'd like to invite you and dad's other friends over for some food? I thought it would feel odd otherwise, not meeting any of them until the funeral itself.'

'That's a great idea.'

'I don't think I'll have the time or energy to organise anything more than home delivery pizza and some beer.'

'It sounds perfect.'

'I thought it would be a nice way for me to put some names to the faces of the people dad cared most about.'

'How about I tell everyone about it? It would save you the time?'

Marsha smiles. 'That would be great, Andy. How many people should I expect?'

'Well, we're nine – sorry, eight in the syndicate. Sorry Marsha, I've still not …'

She touches my hand. 'Easy mistake to make. Shall we say from seven thirty onwards?'

'I'll let everyone know.'

Marsha nods. 'I thought I'd leave the photo albums out, you know, should anyone want to take a look.'

'That's a nice idea.'

'That's settled then.' Marsha smiles at me and I smile back. Her eyes linger. We arrive at the front of the queue. Then she moves in close to me, close enough that I pick up the scent of her perfume. 'It's been so nice, meeting you,' she says, touching my arm with her fingers.

'You too,' I say.

Freed of any inhibitions by the wine perhaps, Marsha

softly kisses me on the mouth. I'm caught off guard and pull away. 'Oh, God,' she says, 'I'm so sorry. I didn't mean to …'

'No,' I say, softly. 'Don't be.'

'My feelings are all over the place,' she says. 'I didn't mean to …'

I take her hand and look her in the eye. 'Marsha, it isn't that I don't find you attractive. It's just ...'

She smiles at me. 'You're already spoken for?'

I nod. 'In fact, any day now I'm going to become a dad.'

'Bloody hell, I am *so* sorry! Please pretend that never happened – and, er - congratulations!'

I smile and look at her. 'It's already forgotten. And thank you.'

* * *

I board the train. I find a half empty carriage and sit down at a window-side seat. Before long, drowsy from the wine, I succumb to the gentle, rhythmic motion as we hurtle through the urban sprawl that is the West Midlands. Before long I nod off, my head nestled into my headrest. When I wake up, I take out my mobile and punch in Rita's number. She picks up on the fourth ring.

How did it go?'

'Fine,' I say, staring out of the window.

'*Did* she give you a hard time?'

'No. I'm glad to say that she didn't.'

'Good. I'm pleased.'

The ticket inspector approaches and I show him my ticket. He punches a hole through its middle. 'How are you feeling?' I ask.

'Oh, you know – *big.'* I picture her in my mind's eye and smile.

'I'll get in to Nottingham Station at around seven.'

'Okay,' she says. 'Well, I'm glad everything went okay.'

'Me too. And I found out some intriguing stuff about Des' past.'

'Really? Sounds interesting,' she says.

'It is. I'll tell you all about it when I get home.'

'Okay. Don't be surprised if I'm asleep when you get in, though.'

'Don't worry. You rest. I just thought I'd ring to say that I'm on my way home.'

'Thanks for letting me know,' she says, yawning.

'And Rita?'

'Yes?'

I hesitate before continuing. 'I love you.'

A brief silence follows. 'I love you too. What brought that on?'

'I don't know. I just thought I should tell you more often.'

42

★ ANDY ★

Turning right outside Nottingham station, I head in the direction of the bus depot beside the Arndale Centre. As I pass the Totesport betting shop, I feel a tap on the shoulder. I turn around. Stood facing me is One-Armed.

'Andy,' he says.

'Alright?' I reply guardedly.

He takes out his cigarettes. 'Smoke?'

'Er, no thanks. I'm trying to give up. You know, little one on the way and all that.'

'Good on you. I gave up and then started again.' A short silence falls over us. 'I heard about Des,' he says.

'Yeah. It's horrible.'

'I can't believe it.'

I nod. 'I've just got back from Birmingham from meeting his daughter.'

'That can't have been easy,' he says adding, 'poor Kyle.'

'Yeah.' I look at my shoes.

'Andy. Do you have time for a quick pint?'

I look at my watch. 'Sure.'

* * *

We head to the Bell Inn on Angel Row. It's less than half full. We order beers at the bar and sit opposite one another at a window table.

'I was out of order,' he says. 'Up in Wolverhampton. I'm sorry.'

'Forget it.'

'No, I owe you an explanation. About why I sneaked more money on Star than what we all agreed to.'

I take a mouthful from my pint and look up at him from my pint glass. 'Okay.'

He takes a deep breath and then slowly exhales. 'It was to try to win enough money to buy a transit van.'

'A transit van?'

'Yeah.'

'Why?'

'In order that I can pack in my security job and take up another offer.'

'Okay.' I take a sip from my pint. 'As what?'

'As a maintenance and service engineer,' says One-Armed.

'Okay. Err, working in what area?'

One-Armed looks suddenly self-conscious. 'Promise me not to laugh when I tell you?'

'Of course,' I say.

'You promise? It's just it's going to sound funny, that's all.'

'C'mon, Bruce. I promise. Just tell me.'

'Okay.' He takes a sip from his pint – and fixes me with his small eyes. 'Maintaining and servicing one-armed-bandits.'

I almost choke on my beer.

'You see? I *knew* you'd laugh!'

'I'm not laughing Bruce! It's just, "like name, like nature" – or whatever the saying is.'

'I know,' he smiles. He takes a mouthful from his pint. 'Do you know who came up with my nickname in the first place?'

'No, I don't as it happens.'

'Des.'

'Really?'

'Yeah. One night at the King Billy. He asked me what I would do, if I could pack in security work?'

'What did you say?'

'I told him that ever since I was a kid, I've been fascinated by one-armed-bandits. It started in Skeggy, on family holidays when I was little. Dad had a mate who worked at an arcade there. When it closed down, he slipped him this fella some money and got hold of an old fruit machine for me. It was going to be slung out. I loved that old thing. I was twelve at the time. I stripped it down in the garage and figured out how it worked.'

I shoot him a smile. 'I don't suppose you ever found the mechanism that triggers a pay out?'

Bruce laughs. 'I wish. I was just a kid. Nowadays I hardly play them. Horses and dogs, that's me, as you know. But dad getting me that old fruit machine triggered my love for them. I guess because they always remind me of happy days as a kid in Skeggy.'

'I think it would be great to change job Bruce and work with something you enjoy.'

He takes a swig of lager. 'Well, a couple of weeks back, Collette noticed a job vacancy in the Nottingham Post. Maintaining and servicing one-armed-bandits, all around the East Midlands. 'You should apply for that,' she said.

'And did you?'

'I did. The interview couldn't have gone any better. It had a practical part. The fella who interviewed me was really impressed with how I knew my way around inside them. He offered me the job there and then.'

'Cool. So, when do you start?'

'Thing is, there was a hitch. He told me I have to provide my own transport; you know – like a transit van? I went home and explained to Collette. A few days later we found one, second hand, but later that week, disaster struck.'

'What happened?'

'Collette got made redundant. With so many fixed outgoings, with just one of us working, we're reluctant to buy anything on HP. Not until she finds another job. That's why I saw the coup as a means of paying for the cost of it.'

'Why didn't you tell me all of this before Star ran?'

He looks down at his hands. 'I did try to - in that Happy Chef on the way to Dunstall Park, but, well – you know, I bottled it.'

'Don't you think I'd have understood if you'd said you wanted to have a bit more on Star than everyone else?' Bruce goes quiet. 'Bruce?'

'Yeah. I know you would have.'

'Just out of interest, how much did you win?'

'About nine grand. It would have been about double that, if Star hadn't dead-heated – not to sound ungrateful. It left me with a bit to find. When I rang the guy to see if the van was still available and if we could work something out, it had gone.'

I take a mouthful of beer. 'This job – is it still yours if you want it?'

'Yeah. Fella said he'd keep it open, though I don't know for how long exactly.'

Bruce looks at his watch and quickly finishes his pint. 'I have to collect the kids. Collette has an interview.'

As we leave the pub, I mention Marsha's 'do' this coming Saturday. 'I'll see you there, yeah?'

'Of course,' he calls out. 'Wouldn't miss it for anything.'

43

★ ANDY ★

Marsha's gathering couldn't have gone better. Before the evening draws to a close, after everyone helped clear away the empty beer cans and pizza cartons, she makes a touching request.

'Thank you all for coming tonight. I can't explain what it means to me, getting to meet all of my dad's mates like this.' Her words are met my a murmur of approval. She pauses briefly before continuing. 'And now that I'm better acquainted with all of you, I feel less awkward about asking a favour of you.'

'Anything,' says Glen.

'Whatever you need,' says Duke.

Marsha approaches Kyle and puts her arm around his shoulder. 'Kyle?' she says.

'Er, yeah, it's like this, see. I need seven pall bearers to help with grandpa's coffin, tomorrow.' He didn't have to ask twice.

* * *

At the funeral, we all get to say our last goodbyes to Des. No one drops their corner of the coffin or slips on their way down the aisle. Marsha makes a moving speech, as does Kyle. It's a sombre and sad occasion – funerals are, of course - but with Des now nothing more than a pile of ash at the bottom of a shiny urn, I'm left struggling to accept that life is simply meant to just carry on without him. *Isn't there some other way we could properly celebrate the life of our friend?*

My train of thought is interrupted by the telephone. I pick up.

'Andy, it's Marsha.'

'Hi, how's things?'

'Not bad thanks. I just rang to ask if you had heard the news from Nine Elms Stables?'

'No. What's that?'

'Ellie has accepted the stable apprentice job.'

'That's great news.'

'It is. And as things turn out, it has repercussions for Kyle, you see.'

'How do you mean?'

'His two-week trial ended a couple of days ago. Ray had already assured him that he'd be required for another four weeks, so that's great. Kyle came home with me for the weekend. Waiting for us when we got back to Birmingham was an envelope on the door mat containing his GCSE results.'

'How did he do?'

'Not so great. The ones he needed to get into technical college in Solihull he failed.'

'I'm sorry, Marsha.'

'I'm not sure he really had his heart set on it. But at the same time, it was the only thing he had lined up once he's finished at Ray's. It really brought things home to him. He got in to a real state. It was a blow, because he's been so happy lately.'

'I'm so sorry, for both of you.'

'I know you are, Andy. Fortunately, our despair was short lived.'

'How do you mean?'

'Well, the following afternoon, Ray rings. Ellie becoming stable jockey created a new vacancy. And with Kyle having impressed during his trial, you'll never guess?'

'What?'

Ray's offered him Ellie's old job full-time!'

'You're kidding …'

'No, I'm not! Ellie is going to train him up, while she takes on rides for the stable.'

'You must be delighted. Not to mention, very proud.'

'I am, especially when I think how proud Des would have been.'

Marsha and I continue to talk for a little while longer, before she has to ring off – and the moment she does, an idea begins to form in my mind.

* * *

'What about running Star again at Dunstall Park next week, Andy? I thought we could attempt a "Mark Prescott", you know – try and run up a sequence of wins?'

I'm sat with my feet up in the living room. And as Ray continues talking, it suddenly strikes me exactly how we should celebrate Des properly, including where I want to run Star next.

'So, what do you think, Andy?' says Ray. But I don't really hear him. 'Andy? Are you still there?'

'Yeah – er, sorry. It's just that I've just had an idea. '

'Okay?' says Ray.

'Have you got a minute while I run it by you?'

PART III

44

★ ANDY ★

A year to the day since making my unsuspecting friends the co-owners of an unraced filly, we return to Nine Elms Stables. As I park the transit van in the courtyard, the sun comes out. I get out and stretch my legs. Glen, Duke, Big Les, the Chans, Rita and One-Armed do the same. Ray, Ellie and Marsha wave to us from the steps of the grey stone cottage. I've told everyone that the purpose of our visit is simply to indulge our Dunstall Park heroine with polo mints, carrots and affection, though I have an ulterior motive for getting everyone together – and having already won Ray over with my plan, the time has come for me to run it by the others.

* * *

We gather in front of the cottage, chatting and laughing with one another. After a while, Ray asks Kyle to lead us all towards the stabling area. As we arrive, I see Star's head bobbing to and frow as we approach her box.

'You've got visitors, girl,' says Kyle, ruffling her mane.

'Bring her out in to the courtyard Kyle, so everyone can enjoy a moment with her,' says Ray.

Kyle nods, unlatches the door to her box and leads her towards us.

'Go easy with the treats, all of you!' jokes Ray.

Everyone gets their turn with Star, stroking her mane and caressing her white blaze. When it's my turn, I peel two mints from a roll of polos and hold them under her mouth. She crunches them up noisily. Her tongue tickles my fingers and when I laugh, she brushes her head against mine and blows. Everyone laughs before Kyle, upon a signal from Ray, leads her back towards her box, before changing his mind.

'Change of plan, Kyle. Bring her along with us instead, yeah?'

'Sure Ray. Where are we heading?'

'We're going to meet Ellie under the big oak tree. You can turn her out in the field next door, the one in the middle of the all-weather gallop. She can graze there today. It'll be a nice change of scenery for her.'

* * *

When we reach the gallops, Kyle releases Star into the field as instructed. The rest of us continue towards the big oak tree. Ellie is sitting underneath it, with her feet up on the long white table, topping up her tan in the afternoon sunshine. When she notices us, she rolls down the sleeves and approaches. She embraces Rita and I in turn. 'Ray says you wanted a word?' she says, shading her face from the sun.

'That's right. Though what I have to say is for everyone, so, please folks - grab a chair and make yourselves comfortable.' Everyone finds a seat and looks back towards me, sat at the head of the table. I clear my throat and smiling broadly, begin. 'Some of you may recall that it was a year ago today that we sat at this very table and drank a toast to Star.'

'Is it really a year ago?' says Big Les.

'It is. That was also the day I first shared my dream with you all – to have Star laid out for a race at Colwick Park.' I pause and take out my cigarettes. 'Unfortunately, that dream never became a reality – though I'm sure you'll agree that her run at Dunstall Park in many ways made up for it.' A murmur of agreement sweeps around the table. I light a cigarette. 'The tragedy of that weekend was, of course, losing our dear friend Des. Ever since his funeral, I've been trying to think of a way in which we could celebrate his life properly – not just of the man we all knew and loved from the bookies, but also in acknowledgement of his achievements as an apprentice jockey, long before we all got to know him.' I pause before continuing. 'Then last week, an idea struck me – and this is what I'd like to share with you today.' A hush falls over the table, before I continue. 'As we learnt from the photo album Marsha recently shared with us, in 1955, Des found himself just one winner short of being crowned Champion Apprentice Jockey of Barbados.' I allow my words to resonate, before turning to address Marsha. 'So, I was wondering, Marsha. Wondering how you would feel about the Manvers Road Star Syndicate sponsoring a race at Colwick Park in Des' honour, here in the town he made his home these past forty years.'

Marsha remains quiet for what seems like an eternity, before eventually breaking her silence. 'I'm speechless,' she says. Rita puts a comforting arm around her shoulder. 'To think that you would like to do this in honour of my dad?'

'I would,' I say. 'I think we'd *all* like to, wouldn't we?' My words are met by a noisy chorus of approval. 'And given that the race would be run in memory of Des, I thought it would be appropriate if the one we sponsor is for apprentice jockeys.'

'Great idea,' says Duke.

'I've looked into the matter and as luck would have it, there is one such race at Colwick Park's final meeting of the season, in a few weeks' time. Then, when I found out that it's a six-furlong race, another idea struck me. I immediately rang Ray for his opinion and after some very careful consideration, we were in agreement.'

'In agreement about what?' says Sammy.

'To run Star.'

'I love it!' shouts Big Les. 'I can see Des now, smiling down at us from the weighing room in the sky!'

'What a cracking idea, Andy!' adds Glen.

The growing sense of excitement is cut short by Ellie. 'Aren't you all forgetting something?' she says.

Ray smiles. 'Her impaired vision?'

'Exactly,' says Ellie.

Ray goes on. 'Neither Andy nor I take the decision to run Star lightly. But at the end of the day, the way I think about it is like this. After Andy put the idea to me, I remembered something that has stuck in my mind from the day Star lost her eye. It was a comment made during a radio programme I heard, about the life of the singer, Ray Charles. What I remembered was the reaction of his mother, upon learning that her seven-year-old boy had lost his sight. Now, just put yourself in her position for a moment. Do you think she was going to allow her son's disability to get in the way of him continuing to learn the piano? Of course not. And though her son had lost one of his four senses, it wasn't long before he began compensating with the ones he still had. I believe it is in our DNA as human beings - an inner determination to make the most of our abilities, whatever cards we are dealt in life and I believe that thoroughbreds are the same. While Star will never be good enough to win a Group One race at Royal Ascot, no one can deny the sheer courage and bravery she showed us at Dunstall Park in overcoming her disability.'

Duke sparks up. 'Nicely put, Ray.'

Ray continues. 'We can speculate until the cows come home about whether she will handle a straight six furlongs on turf or not – or get spooked again when she sees an oncoming rival late on her blind right side. Only Star herself will be able to tell us – and she can only do *that* if we let her take her chance.'

I allow Ray's words to resonate, before turning to face Ellie. I change tact. 'I believe congratulations are in order?'

'Huh?' she says.

'A little bird told me that you've accepted Ray's offer to become his apprentice jockey?'

'That's right,' she replies, blushing.

'Congratulations, Ellie,' I say.

'Thank you.'

I turn and address everyone. 'A round of applause for Nine Elms Stables' new apprentice jockey!' Ellie's face turns an even deeper shade as the applause ring out – and when the clapping dies down, I strike. 'You see, Ellie - Ray and I were wondering something.'

'Wondering what?' she says.

'If *you* would take the ride on Star at Colwick Park?'

Eleven faces hone in on her. 'Bloody hell! I – er …'

'After all, like Des always said, no one knows Star better than you do,' I say.

'He said that?'

I nod. 'He also said you have what racing people refer to as "good hands."'

'Really?'

'Yes. Though when he said it, I didn't know they were the words of a man who had ridden over twenty winners at Garrison Savannah Racecourse!' Everyone laughs.

Ray pipes up. 'Andy's not telling porkies, Ellie. The last time I heard Des say no one knows Star better than you do, was a couple of days before she ran at Dunstall Park.'

'That's right,' I say.

Ray goes on. 'I reckon Des felt *you* should have got the ride ahead of Seb Sanders!'

Ellie still looks as though she is in two minds. I up the ante. 'Think about it for a moment. How cool would it be? Your first ride as a professional jockey, on a horse that has been in your care since the first day she came into training here?'

Duke chips in. 'With the chance of, metaphorically speaking, riding Des his apprentice title clinching ride, all these years later?'

Ellie's reaction is immediate. 'That is exactly what puts me off,' she says. 'The expectations you're going to have of me!'

'Wait a minute,' I say. 'I don't think Duke meant it like that.'

Ellie isn't listening. 'While I know that part of becoming a professional jockey will be having to learn to live with carrying owners' money as well as their hopes, I – '

'Ellie,' I gently cut her short. 'Landing a load of hefty bets on our behalf isn't what this race is going to be about.'

'But –', she starts.

I cut her short again. 'If making a quick buck from Star's next run was our priority, I would have gone with Ray's suggestion - to run her back at Dunstall Park.' I let my words resonate, before continuing. 'Ever since her first run Ellie, everything about Star has been a team effort.'

'How do you mean?' she says.

'Well, just getting her to Southwell for her debut involved input from several of us. Sure, I was lucky enough to have the money to buy her, but it was Laura who suggested Ray here to find us a good one, not to mention, train her.' I turn and point at Big Les. 'And it was this fella here who was responsible for coming up with her brilliant name.' Big Les blushes, as I approach Duke and rest my hand on his shoulder. 'Duke here took care of the legal side of things, like registering her name and forming a syndicate - and then there was the Chans contribution,' I say smiling.

Ellie looks intrigued. 'How were you and your dad, involved, Sammy?' she says.

'By designing the silks,' he replies proudly. Lee Chan bows graciously at the recognition afforded them.

'Getaway!' says Ellie.

'Yeah - straight up,' says Sammy.

I soldier on. 'Star's next run can be another team effort, but with a couple of additional key members.' I hesitate before continuing. 'If *you* agree to take the ride Ellie, there's another person we'll need to complete the line-up.' I look at the person sat to Marsha's left.

'Kyle?' I say.

'Yes?'

'Would you do us the honour of leading Ellie and Star in the parade ring?'

Kyle's face lights up and his immediate acceptance of my offer has the desired knock-on effect. 'Ellie?' Kyle says.

'All right, all right, all right!' she says. 'I'll do it!'

* * *

Spirits are high in the transit van as I pull out of Nine Elms Stables. I drop Bruce and Glen off on the way back into town. Everyone else gets out on Manvers Road. As I park the rental van on the car dealership forecourt just around the corner, an idea comes to me - and following a chat with the dealership owner, I return to the vehicle and drive to small terraced house half way along the Basford Road. I park up and knock on the door to number twenty-four. The door opens. 'Oh, hi, Andy?' says Bruce. 'What are you doing here?'

Two small children poke their heads around Bruce's legs and gaze up at me. I point at the transit van parked up on the curb outside his house.

'Will that do?' I say smiling.

Bruce looks confused. 'How do you mean?' He looks down at his children. 'Go inside, you two. Tell your mum I'll be in in a minute.' The two children scurry inside.

'For your new job, I mean? The seats fold down in the back and everything.'

Bruce joins me on the curb outside his small house. 'Well, yeah. It's exactly what I need – but I don't follow you.'

'Good,' I say, handing him the keys. 'Then she's yours.'

Bruce is dumbfounded. *'What?'*

'Do you want to hear a funny story about that transit van?'

Bruce nods, evidently still stunned.

'When I returned that very same van after Star made her debut at Southwell last year, the manager of the car dealership asked me if I wanted to make him an offer on it? Though I didn't say anything at the time, I think he'd mixed me up with someone else who had shown an interest. Anyway, whenever I've hired it since, I've sort of played along, knocking his price down a bit each time he suggested a price.

Well, half-an-hour ago, he accepted an offer that I found was just too good to pass up.'

'How much did he want?' says Bruce anxiously.

'To you, mate, nothing.'

'What?'

'She's yours.'

'I can't just ...'

'Look at it as an overdue "commission" - for helping my dad place that winning bet last year. After all, if for whatever reason he hadn't got it on, I'd never have been able to buy us Star, would I?'

'Andy ...'

'Bruce, it's cool. It's pointless arguing with me. This way, the money you won on Star can be a buffer for you and Collette until she finds another job.'

Bruce is a big fella - but when I look at him, he suddenly looks as innocent and vulnerable as his two kids. Tears of relief fill his eyes. 'I don't know what to say?' He lunges at me and holds me in such a strong bear hug, that for a moment I think I'm going to pass out.

'There's nothing *to* say, Bruce – but there are a couple of things you need to do?'

'What's that?' he says, releasing me from his grip.

'Ring that fella immediately and take the job he offered you. And when you've done that, ring your boss at the security company and tell him where to stick his job!'

* * *

Two days later, I'm sat opposite Laura in her office at Colwick Park. On her desk is a pop-up 1997 Jockey Club Racecourse Calendar and a potted cactus. The best feature of the room is the view from her office window of the parade ring, less than fifty yards away.

'So, which of those that I read out do you think works best?' I say.

'Read that last one back to me again, would you?' she says, stirring her cup of tea.

I look down at the sheet of A4 sheet of paper in front of me. 'Okay,' I reply, clearing my throat. 'The Demond James 1955 Champion Apprentice Jockey of Barbados Memorial Handicap.'

Laura's reaction is immediate. 'That's the one! And to keep it that length, we can put the 'Class Five, six-furlong race for apprentice jockeys,' underneath in smaller print.

'Great!' I say. 'I'll run it by Marsha and get back to you.'

Laura nods. 'And if she'd like a few lines in the programme about Des as well as a photo of him, then get her to ring me, okay?'

45

★ MARSHA ★

Three weeks before the race in dad's honour, I book two flights to Barbados out of the money he won. Having accepted his new full-time position, Kyle was able to negotiate some time off with Ray. Kyle loves life at Nine Elms Stables, free from the toxic confines of school. Del and I couldn't be happier for him, though I have put my foot down by making him re-sit his English and Maths GCSE's, offering to pay for a few hours' private tuition nearer the time. That said, Ray's offer to teach him to drive seems of far more practical use to him right now than two paper certificates.

* * *

As our holiday approaches, the only regret I have is that we're making the trip to Barbados without mum and dad. I find this as sad as it is ironic, though this feeling lessens after I discover something in the living room one day. Underneath the glass topped table, hidden beneath a pile of old magazines, I find an A6 size envelope. Written on the cover in dad's handwriting are the words 'Barbados, 1991. Places to show Marsha and Kyle.' There hadn't been a holiday to Barbados that year, of course - though clearly it had been dad's intention. I recall the evening he'd made me Bajan Stew in Nottingham; and how he'd said something about how close he'd come, a few years back, to paying for us all to go.

As I sit down on the sofa, it occurs to me how the envelope most likely got there – escaping Kyle's attention as he'd gathered the loose papers that had fallen out of the back of dad's album, the evening Andy rang. I leave the envelope on the table and fetch a glass of wine from the fridge. Returning to the sofa, I pick it up and study it. I go to open it, but something makes me change my mind and I leave it on a pile of items that include our holiday documents and passports instead.

46

★ ANDY ★

It's September and the football season is in full swing. My lot, The Pies, begin the season newly relegated to Division Three. By the time I get along to see them, the signs of a direct return to Division Two look hopeful. Our new manager, Sam Allardyce, has us playing a more direct style, better suited to life in the Third. It's paying early dividends and going into this afternoon's game against Scarborough United, we've won five and drawn two of our opening eight games.

* * *

On my way to the Navigation Inn, I recall the last time I saw them - a wet Tuesday evening, two days after dad died. It wasn't until the very last minute that I decided to go on my own. We usually went to home games with Dave and Rob, former miners like dad from Cotgrave Colliery. But that evening I wanted to be just for dad for me, so I didn't ring them. I stood on my own on the terraces in the rain and cried my eyes out at the end of the game. It wasn't the result that upset me – we won, 1-0 – more the delayed realisation, at the sound of the final whistle, that I'd never see The Pies play with dad again. I took a break from going after that. I figured Dave and Rob would understand. Besides, I'd just started seeing Rita, not long before Duke and Laura invited us to Colwick Park, a short while before I bought Star.

* * *

Around a week before Star's run at Colwick Park, I ring Dave and Rob about going to the game with them. Dad would definitely have approved me asking and fortunately they both say yes.

'Dave!' I call out, spotting him as I enter the pub.

'All right, Youth!' He puts down his pint glass and gives me a hug. Dave has aged since I last saw him, but the mischievous sparkle in his eyes is still there.

'Good to see you,' I say. 'How's things?'

'Can't complain like. And you?'

'I'm good. Still at The Post, though I do have some exciting news.'

'Oh yeah? And what's that then?' he says.

'I'm about to became a dad.'

'Getaway! This calls for a celebration! What are you having?'

'No, I'll get them in. I insist. Pint of Shipstones?'

'Yeah, alright. Cheers, Andy.'

'Same for Rob?' Dave nods. 'By the way,' I say, 'where *is* Rob?'

'He's taking a slash. Problems with his waterworks. Must be his age.' Dave laughs. I join in. As the barman pulls our pints, I turn around and there he is, on his way over from the gents. He's wearing his trademark donkey jacket, his Notts

County scarf hanging loose around his neck. Rob beams brightly upon seeing me. 'Alright, Youth?' He gives me a hug.

I pass him his pint. 'Not bad. And you?'

'Andy's got some news, haven't you?' says Dave.

Rob takes a mouthful of beer. 'What's that then?'

'Yeah, I was just telling Dave. I'm about to become a dad.'

'Bloody hell, congratulations!'

'Are you nervous?' says Dave.

I take a sip from my pint. 'I'm terrified.' I take a swig of lager.

'How do you mean?' says Rob.

'Scared, you know. Of messing it up - fatherhood and that.' I check Dave's reaction. He just smiles, not the reaction I'd expected. 'What is it?' I say.

'No,' he says. 'It's just that you remind me of someone, that's all.'

'Who?'

'Your dad. When you were on the way.'

* * *

That afternoon, following a 2-1 win, The Pies go top of Division Three. As the three of us file out of Meadow Lane, we make arrangements to meet ahead of the next home game. Seeing Rob and Dave again puts me in great spirits - but my mood changes as I turn onto Sneinton Boulevard, when I see an ambulance, siren wailing and orange lights flashing, pull over in front of Sanjays. My eyes scale the stairway leading to the flat and stood at the top, I see Rita. My heart skips a beat and I burst into a sprint.

Two paramedics jump out of the ambulance. Climbing the

stairway, I watch as they assist Rita to street level – and as I pull up outside the entrance to Sanjays, hands on knees and gasping for breath, she looks me in the eyes.

'Andyyyy! This time it's for real!'

* * *

Two years to the day after vowing to leave Sneinton for good - and around a year since Rita gave me reason to rethink and stay - I become a dad. And from the moment Rita's midwife delivers little Grace into my arms, any lingering fears I harboured about becoming a parent evaporate into thin air. I plant myself on the edge of the bed, holding the small bundle in my arms for all its worth. I look at Rita and smile. 'You did it, Rita.'

'No. *We* did it, Andy,' she says.

47

★ MARSHA ★

'Are you soon ready, love?'

'A couple of minutes, yeah?' says Kyle.

I'm sat in our hotel room on our first morning in Barbados. The whir of the air conditioning fan is working over-time above my head.

I remove dad's envelope from my handbag. I open it impatiently. Inside are three pages of A4 paper, folded twice. There's writing on both sides. I straighten them out and take a look. It's a handwritten list of places mum and dad had planned to show us. The notes under each place vary in length, from a couple of sentences to a couple of paragraphs.

Kyle appears before me. 'Ready mum.'

I look up and smile. 'Hungry?' I say.

'Yeah. You?'

I nod. 'C'mon, let's go.'

* * *

I resist reading all of dad's notes in one go. Instead, I read his words out loud to Kyle, as we go along. It has the magical effect of making both mum and dad seem present everywhere we go, such as on a walking tour of Bridgetown, at the cemetery where Grandpa James is buried and at Moe's Place, the oldest fish shack on the island who, according to dad's notes, "make the best fish cutter sandwiches in all of Barbados."

'How would you like them, darling?' asks the elderly man behind the counter. Kyle smiles as I consult dad's notes and paraphrase.

'"Top each of the salt buns with mayo,"' please,' I say.

'Sure,' he says.

'"Lay a slice of tomato on the bottom, the lettuce leaves next and then the fillet of fish."'

The elderly man looks at me. 'Perhaps a little Cheddar Cheese?' asks the man politely. I look at him with an uncertain smile and quickly consult dad's notes. 'Er, yes please – "and drizzle plenty of Bajan Pepper sauce over it."'

'Traditional style - I like it!' laughs the man. Kyle and I join in his laughter as he completes our order.

* * *

Nowhere do Kyle and I feel mum and dad's presence more than at Garrison Savannah Racecourse. I recite dad's entry about the place as we approach the grandstand. '"Let's eat at the restaurant where you mother used to work,"' writes dad – '"and leave a generous tip, like the very best customers!"'

Kyle and I are shown to a table overlooking the plush, green home straight by our waitress, who introduces herself as Marcia. After ordering drinks and placing our order, I find myself watching her and her colleagues, as they work the restaurant floor. For a moment I imagine a mid-twenties' version of mum: cordial and attentive with her guests, while all the time secretly longing for the end of her shift and a date with dad at Pebbles Beach. The food is good, as is the service and after settling the bill, I conceal a twenty- dollar note discreetly under my place mat. We make to leave. 'Don't forget your rucksack, Kyle,' I say.

* * *

We carefully descend the wooden stairs of the grandstand and emerge into the harsh afternoon sunlight. Kyle turns and faces me. 'So where to next?'

'You don't mind grandpa's notes, do you?' I say.

'No, Mum. They're great.'

'Oh, good. I think so too.' I send Kyle a broad smile. 'Okay, let's see.' I slip my sunglasses down over my eyes. 'So, next dad writes, "be sure to show Marsha and Kyle the paddock. It's the most tranquil place on the racecourse. It's pretty too, lined with shrubs and richly scented flowers unique to Barbados. It's also the best place to see the horses up close."

I look at Kyle. He nods approvingly. Pointing at a wooden signpost, he says, 'Look. This way.'

Kyle and I lean casually against the white rails along the side of the paddock, shaded from the sun, race day programmes in hand. The horses arrive for the next race, led up by their grooms. It's humid. The air is thin, though fragrant with scented flowers. I remove a flask of water from my bag and take a sip. Kyle and I watch the horses pass by in silence. Some are skitty and jumpy, others not so, calmly taking in their surroundings.

'Look,' says Kyle, pointing. 'Here come the jockeys.'

We watch as they fan into the paddock from the centre of the course. By the looks of it, they're all native Bajan - lean and well-trained, resplendent in their colourful, shiny silks.

As I watch the last jockey receive a leg up onto his horse, I feel dad's presence. The jockey's silks are a distinctive tangerine orange and sky-blue colour and he wears a sky-blue cap. I consult my programme. Number five on the race card. Horse and jockey are led directly in front of Kyle and I. I look into the jockey's eyes and ever so briefly, see a younger version of dad. 'Good luck,' I say.

'Thank you,' says the jockey, in a soft Bajan tone, not unlike dad's.

I turn to Kyle. 'Shall we have a bet?'

He smiles. 'Sure. Which one do you like?'

I scan my race card. 'The one that was just led past. Number five. Bajan Rose. And you?'

'I don't know. They all look good to me. Let's double up on your one.'

'Okay,' I say. 'This is fun, isn't it?'

Kyle laughs. 'Yeah, it is. C'mon, let's go and get our money on before it's too late.'

As the runners and riders arrive at the start, Kyle and I hurry inside the grandstand to join the queue at the tote counter.

* * *

The sound of thundering hooves becomes louder. The ground begins to tremor beneath our feet. The atmosphere around us is electrifying. Kyle and I jump up and down excitedly beside the finishing post, about three rows back, willing Bajan Rose home. Neither of us can see much - and the commentary is delivered at such speed and in such a strong Bajan accent, it offers little in the way of clues about Bajan Roses' progress in the closing stages. A gap in the crowd appears in front of us, just as the winning horse flashes past … in a blur of orange and sky blue!

'I don't believe it! He won, Kyle! Bajan Rose won!'

'Yeesss!' Kyle punches the air, before the two of us lock in an embrace, laughing uncontrollably.

* * *

Ten minutes later, one hundred and twenty dollars wealthier, Kyle and I are carried along by the crowd towards the race-course exit. Briefly consulting dad's notes, I stop and read the next entry. The heading reads "Pebbles Beach." I turn to a man around the same age as myself, stood at the racecourse gates. He's dressed in a Hawaiian shirt, dark shades and a red baseball cap, worn back to front.

'Excuse me. Do you know how we get to Pebbles Beach from here?' I say.

The man smiles. 'Turn left outside the gates and head along the gravel road. Just keep walking. You can't miss it.'

I thank him - and while most of our fellow racegoers take a right turn back towards Bridgetown, Kyle and I set off towards the beach.

* * *

At the end of the gravel road, the final one hundred yards take a slight uphill incline, enhancing the visual impact one experiences upon reaching the beach. We take in the view.

'Wow,' says Kyle.

'First impressions?' I say.

Kyle turns to face me. 'If there's such a place as paradise on earth, Mum, then this has to be it.' I burst into laughter. 'What's so funny?' he says.

'It's just uncanny, that's all. Those are the exact words your grandpa used to describe this place, whenever we looked through his red photo album together.' Kyle smiles. I go on. 'This was their favourite place on the whole island, Kyle - the place they always came to when your grandma got off work and dad had ridden his last race.' We stand there in silence, drinking in the view. Gradually my favourite photograph of mum and dad comes to life before my eyes; dad sat beside mum with his arm around her, the white sandy beach rolling out from beneath their toes, down to the calm turquoise waters of the North Atlantic Ocean. A line of white dots, distant sailing boats, speckle the horizon, above which the ocean fades seamlessly into a cloudless blue sky. To our right, the curry-yellow pier with the leaf green roof and elegant white terracing juts out into the sea – and to our left, the beach winds around the bay for what looks like miles.

* * *

Four giant thoroughbreds pass by, led by their grooms towards the beach. One of the grooms, his hair platted in stubby dreads, acknowledges us with a smile. Kyle turns and faces me.

'Are those horses being taken for a swim?' he says.

I look at him and smile. 'They are.'

'You didn't say anything about that!' Kyle says.

'No,' I say, playfully pulling him close. 'I wanted it to be a surprise.'

'Cool,' he says.

I notice a cold drinks vendor, half way towards the pier. I doubt it's the same place dad used to buy drinks, but it feels nice, imagining that it could be. I remove a ten-dollar bill from our winnings. 'How about buying us a couple of cold drinks, Kyle? Then we can go and watch the horses bathe.'

He takes the bill and smiles. 'What would you like?'

'A light beer if they have one.'

Kyle nods. 'Can you take my rucksack?'

'Sure,' I reply, removing it from his back. 'I'll be further down towards the sea.'

As Kyle sets off in the direction of the pier, I kick off my sandals, pick them up and stroll barefoot through the sand.

* * *

I put Kyle's rucksack down and stare out to sea.

'Here you go,' he says, reappearing, handing me a bottle of cold beer.

'Thanks.' We clink our bottles together, my beer and his Seven Up. 'You arrived just in time,' I say pointing. 'Look.'

The four grooms begin coaxing their charges in to the sea, by splashing water against their legs, as one would do with a small child. Not long passes before the horses plunge into the water and start swimming. Before long, all that can be seen of them is four heads, bobbing up and down in tandem with their respective groom. When they are out as far as the end of the pier, Kyle and I lie down on the sand with our drinks. I take out dad's notes. I notice that it is his final entry. 'Grandpa begins, "Welcome to Pebbles Beach!"'

Kyle takes a sip of his drink and smiles.

He goes on, '"I heard they've put up a couple of big hotels since your mum and I left. It seems a pity, though I guess it's good for the local economy. In our day, there were no fish shacks or restaurants - just the pier and a drinks vendor, selling beer and soda to local passing trade. Paradise on earth, we used to call it." What did I tell you, Kyle?'

Kyle smiles. I continue reading. '"Shirelle and I have so many memories tied to this place. It's where we got to know each other, the place where we slowly learnt to share our dreams with one another. And when things became more serious between us, it also became the place where we planned our future together. "'I stop and smile. 'Your grandpa writes so well, doesn't he?' Kyle nods. I take a swig of lager and continue. '"But not every memory we have of Pebbles Beach is a happy one - like the last evening we were here, a few days before Hurricane Janet struck."' I look up from the page and glance at Kyle, before reading on. '"The evening, your mum told me she'd …' I stop reading out loud - and complete the sentence in my head.

'What did he write, Mum?' says Kyle.

I look up and slowly say the words out loud. '"Miscarried."' I resume reading out loud. There can be no secrets from Kyle. '"That evening, your mum and I left this place under a dark cloud, uncertain whether we would ever be able to start a family. You see, your mum had miscarried once before."' Kyle and I look at one another in silence, before I continue. '"'Just imagine then how a few years later, four thousand miles away in Nottingham, how blessed we felt when you arrived, Marsha? And some years later after that, when you made us the happiest grandparents on earth, with the arrival of Kyle."' I stop reading, as the impact of dad's words hit home. Kyle moves in close and puts his arms around me. For a while we just sit there in the sand, softly crying together. We remain like that for some time, oblivious to one of the grooms returning from the ocean with his horse.

'Everything okay?' he says.

Shielding the sun from my eyes, I look up. It's the guy with the stubby dreads. I wipe away my tears and smile. 'Thank you. Really, we're fine.'

The man smiles. 'So long as you're sure?'

'Quite sure,' I say. 'We're feeling happy and sad at the same time. Family stuff, you know …'

The man nods and smiles, and slowly continues on his way.

'You okay, Kyle?' I say, ruffling his hair.

'Yeah. Yeah, I'm fine. It was just …'

'Overwhelming?'

'Yeah. Something like that.' I hug him again tightly. Kyle looks me in the eyes. 'You never knew, did you, Mum? About grandma miscarrying?'

'No. No, I didn't.' For a moment we just sit beside one another in silence. After a short while, I say, 'I think it's probably time now, Kyle, don't you?' He nods. In silence he gets to his feet and undoes the top of his rucksack. Carefully he removes two urns; the one from the mantelpiece at dad's house in Nottingham and the other more recent one, containing dad's ashes.

'I have an idea, Mum,' Kyle says.

'Okay.'

'You scatter grandma's ashes and I scatter grandpas?' he says.

'All right.' I look out towards the ocean. The remaining three horses and their grooms are still some distance out.

Kyle looks around. 'Shall we scatter them here on the beach?' he says.

'We could. Or we could scatter them in the sea?'

'I think that's a better idea,' says Kyle.

We walk down to the water's edge and slowly wade into the sea. The water is soothing, warm and transparent. We stop when it reaches our knees. 'Before we start Kyle, I just want to say a few words.'

Kyle looks at me. He nods. 'Sure.'

I take a deep breath and slowly exhale. 'Thank you, Dad. Thank you for making it possible for Kyle and I to visit this magical place. I know just how much it meant to you and mum that we got to come here. And while it's true that Kyle and I made the journey over from England without you, thanks to your notes, we've felt your presence everywhere we've been.' I glance across at Kyle. He nods. 'So, Dad. Something occurred to Kyle and I before we left England - something we felt we could do for you and mum in return and that is, to re-unite you here at your very favourite place.' I remove the cap to the urn containing mum's ashes. Kyle does the same with dad's. I make eye-contact with Kyle. I say, 'on the count of three, yeah?'

'Okay,' says Kyle.

'One, two, three …'

We release the contents of the urns simultaneously. There is little wind and the ashes intermingle. Kyle and I watch them rise, fall and mix; before they disappear like gold dust into the turquoise ocean.

48

★ ANDY ★

Today is a big day for two reasons. The first reason is that Grace is three weeks old today and later, Rita and I will be taking her outside the confines of the flat for the first time. The second reason today is a big day is that Star will finally fulfil my dream by running at Colwick Park. Early afternoon, Rita and I make our way slowly down the stairway past the entrance to Sanjays – Rita clutching Grace and me struggling with the pram. I just about manage to get it down to street level in one piece.

Rita turns and looks at me. 'That was a nightmare. How am I going to manage that, two or three times a day on my own?'

'I know what we should do,' I say.

'What?' she says, carefully lifting Grace into the pram.

'Take mum and dad's house off the market and move in there for a while.'

Rita's face lights up. 'That would be perfect.'

I nod and smile. 'I'll ring the estate agents tomorrow.'

* * *

I push the pram through the gates to St Nicholas Church cemetery, with Rita's arm linked in mine. Two bouquets of flowers lay in the storage section under the pram. The sun is shining and there's a gentle breeze. I park the pram at the end of the bench, across the pathway from mum and dad's gravestones. Rita peers into the pram. 'She's sound asleep. It seems silly to disturb her just yet, don't you think?'

I nod. 'Besides, there's no mad rush with the family introductions,' I add, with a dark smile. Rita shakes her head. I sit down on the bench. Rita joins me. I put my arm around her shoulder and she leans into me.

'This is nice, isn't it?' she says.

'Yeah, it is.' A short silence falls over us – not the awkward kind, a calm, contented one. 'Somethings just occurred to me,' I say.

'What's that?'

'This is the first time we've sat up here together.' Grace stirs. She starts crying.

'Someone's hungry,' says Rita. I fetch Grace's bottle of formula. Rita takes Grace into her arms and begins feeding her. Within seconds, Grace stops crying. 'I think now is probably as good a time as any, don't you?' says Rita.

'Sure,' I say. Suddenly it occurs to me;-how good it feels to be sat on this bench, not just with Rita, but the three of us. A family, a family of my own. I fetch the bouquets and the three of us cross the pathway to the foot of mum and dad's graves. I sweep away some stray leaves and twigs and lay a bouquet at the foot of each one.

'Here, Andy.' Rita passes Grace into my arms.

'Thank you.' I hesitate briefly to formulate my words. 'Mum, Dad - Rita and I have come up here today to introduce to you someone very special. Your first grand-daughter, little Grace Marie here.' I glance at Rita and she sends me a smile.

'I'm so sorry that you never got the chance to meet her while you were both alive. But you can rest assured that she will be raised with the same love and care that you bestowed upon me.' I feel Rita squeeze my hand. I kiss her and then we walk slowly back to the pram.

* * *

Rita stands on the door step to the flat holding Grace in her arms. 'Have a great time, Andy. Don't forget to say hi to everyone from me.'

'Thanks. I will. And as soon as this little one is old enough, the three of us can go to Colwick Park together, can't we?'

'Of course,' she says. 'By the way, I hope you feel proud of yourself?'

'How do you mean?'

Arranging this day. For Des?' she says. I nod and smile. Rita smiles back. 'You'd better get going. You don't want to be late.'

I look at my watch. 'I'll be fine. I'll ring you after the race.'

49

★ ELLIE ★

I approach the Weighing Room building, my kit bag in one hand and tack in another. An elderly jockey club official greets me outside.

'This way, Miss McGovern,' he says, reading my name from the race day programme.

'Thank you.' I grow a couple of inches in height at being referred to by name. He leads me inside, towards a corridor to the left of the weighing room scales.

'It's along there,' he says, smiling. I reciprocate.

The corridor is narrow and dimly lit. A chipped white door awaits me at its far end. An A4 sheet of paper is taped to it with the words 'Lady Jockeys Changing Room' printed on it. I turn the door handle and enter and scan the small, windowless room. My silks and cap hang from a clothes hook on the facing wall above a short bench. Butterflies flutter in my tummy. A hand basin stands against the near wall, besides an unmounted full-length mirror. I put my kit bag down on to the bench, unzip it and take out my mobile phone. I bite my lip anxiously as I tap the screen and sigh. *'No new messages.'*

* * *

A few minutes later I'm dressed. I stand in front of the full-length mirror and study my reflection. If they'd had had their way, I would be dressed in a sharp business suit, working in an office with my name on the door. Instead, I study *my* uniform of choice - jockey silks, cap, britches and boots: my *battle dress.* The five years that have led to this moment flash through my mind. Bunking off uni to ride out, turning my back on a career in banking and doing my best to ignore the sexist sneers and doubters about my height. Crossing the Irish Sea, finding work at Ray's and getting to know Star. My thoughts are halted by a knock on the door.

'Miss McGovern?'

It's the jockey club official from earlier. 'Yes?' I say.

'It's time,' he says.

'Thank you.'

This is it.

* * *

I take a few strides along the corridor. My mobile phone starts ringing in the changing room, willing me back. I stop in my tracks. *Could that be them*?

The man turns around and looks at me.

'I've just received a – thing is, it might be …'

'Probably just a good luck message, don't you think?' he smiles.

'Probably,' I say, quickly gathering my thoughts. *If it was them, then great,* I think to myself. *I can return the call later. And if it wasn't them*, I reason, *then what does it really matter? What matters is that I'm here, doing this - for me.*

'Miss McGovern?' the man says gently.

'Sorry,' I say. 'I just needed a moment.'

He looks at me kindly. 'It's fine,' he says. 'All good?'

'Yes. All good,' I say, returning his smile.

* * *

As I follow him along the corridor, I try to run through the way I think the race will unfold in my mind. But I'm not Richard Hughes and I fail. As I pass the weighing scales, I focus on what I *do* know: the importance of jumping Star out of the gate fast and making a beeline for the inside rail - stealing a march on Fingal's Cave, City Lights and Pat's Choice, the likely market leaders, all drawn on Star's blind side. From there, I'll improvise. Only then will I discover how much Star has learnt; not just from those early, tentative rehab sessions, but since her run at Dunstall Park.

* * *

I step out into the afternoon sunshine and latch myself on to the tail end of the other apprentices. Reaching the parade ring entrance, we hover in a group, waiting for a gap between parading horses inside. Eventually one comes and we enter.

The parade ring is huge. It's bordered along one side by the tallest row of poplar trees I have ever seen. The butterflies in my tummy return and my legs turn to jelly. I take a deep breath. I look around in need of a familiar face. I don't see any. Apparitions from my past invade my present. All I see are sneering faces, owners and trainers whispering to one another, 'who's that tall *girl* jockey?'

'Ellie!'

I'm saved by Kyle. I look in the direction of his voice and there he is, leading Star out of the parade line towards me.

She looks immaculate – ears pricked, alert, race fit. Kyle stops in front of me. He's dressed in a stylish, linen suit and he's had his afro trimmed. He smiles at me through a pair of stylish dark shades.

'Looking good, Kyle,' I say, giving him a hug.

'You too.'

We both laugh. I ruffle Star's mane. 'Hello beautiful,' I say.

'Check this out,' says Kyle, pointing at his tie. 'Green and red. To go with your silks,' he says.

Something occurs to me. How completely unrecognisable Kyle is to the bashful fellow I first met, just a few months back. 'That's so cool,' I say smiling. 'How was Barbados?'

'Unreal. Did you know that the grooms there bathe their horses in the ocean after racing?'

'Wow. No, I didn't.' Despite Kyle's presence, my butterflies return with a vengeance. 'Are you nervous?' I say.

'A bit. You?'

'No,' I say. 'I'm absolutely shitting myself!' We burst into laughter.

'Ellie, you're going to be fine. It's like Grandpa said. 'No-one knows Star better than you do. Look. There they are!' he says, lifting up his shades, pointing.

* * *

'Here they come,' says Big Les as we approach. Beside him stands Ray, The Chans, Duke, Big Les, Glen, One-Armed Bruce and Marsha. Marsha looks stunning. I take a look around.

'Where are Andy and Rita?' I say.

'Rita is at home with Grace,' says Ray.

'Of course …'

'But Andy is cutting it fine,' he says, checking his watch.

Ding-ding-ding-ding-ding!

* * *

A voice booms over the parade ring tannoy. 'Jockeys please mount. Jockeys, please mount for the Desmond James 1955 Champion Apprentice Jockey of Barbados Memorial Handicap.'

I find myself stood beside Marsha. I watch as she discreetly wipes a tear from her eye. 'Kyle, over here!' she calls, waving a disposable camera in the air. Kyle hands Star's reins to Ray and joins us. Marsha looks at Big Les. 'Would you mind taking a picture of me with my handsome son?'

'It would be an honour,' he says. Big Les steps forward and does the honours. Marsha turns to me and touches my hand. 'Best of luck, Ellie,' she says.

'Thanks Marsha.' I give her a hug. 'This ride is for your dad.'

Marsha hugs me tightly. Kyle pulls Star upsides. Ray gives me a leg up. Then the two of them walk me to the chute leading to the six-furlong start. Ray stops Star before letting us go. 'Ellie?' he says, looking up at me.

'I know, Ray. Jump her out of the gate and angle her straight to the inner rail.'

'Yes, 'he says. 'But I just wanted to wish you good luck.' Ray holds my eye contact and squeezes my hand.

'Oh,' I say. 'Thanks Ray.' I squeeze his hand back.

'Now, go out there and show them all, yeah?' he says.

50

★ ANDY ★

HALF AN HOUR EARLIER

I unlock the door to dad's old Ford Escort and get in. I open the car CD player and slot my disc into the tray, press close, select track five and press 'play.' Within minutes I'm cruising along Sneinton Boulevard with the car windows rolled down. 'What I Say, Parts One and Two' plays out of the car speakers. It's a sunny Nottingham afternoon and all is right in the world. Singing along with Ray, I re-live the feeling of pure joy I felt back in May, upon learning that Star's career wasn't over after all. I drive on through Sneinton's backroads, tapping on the car roof in time to the music. Up ahead lies the A612 turn off, after which it's a clear run all the way to the racecourse. Instead, I find myself slowing to a crawl behind a coachful of seething West Brom *Ultras.* With the Pies playing away and the distraction of Star's race, there is something I've overlooked – Star's race gets underway at exactly the same time as Forest's game against West Brom at the City Ground.

A mass of mocking faces peer at me from the coach rear window. I do my best to ignore their throat slitting mimes and *'wanker'* gestures. I do this by tapping my fingers on the steering wheel and avoiding eye-contact. Having my big day jeopardised by a Notts Forest game is bad - but actually being mistaken for a Forest fan is more than I can bare. Spotting dad's old black and white Pies scarf on the back seat, I grab it and thrust it defiantly against the inside of the windscreen. Peeping around the corner of the scarf, I see their jeers and gestures turn to applause and noticing a gap in the on-coming traffic, I pull out and overtake the coach. I put my foot down and continue towards the A612. *Not far now.* But as I reach the turn off, my heart sinks. There's chock-a-block traffic for as far as I can see. I bang my hands on the steering wheel in frustration. 'Bloody Forest!'

* * *

I abandon dad's car and run towards the next right turn, Eyre Street. I run the length of Eyre Street which leads on to Manvers Road. I run past the King Billy and fighting for breath, arrive at the bookies. I rest my hands on my knees and slowly catch my breath just inside the doorway. My mobile phone starts ringing. I take it out and press answer.

'Where are you?' It's Duke.

'Forest are playing at home aren't they! I got stuck in match day traffic!'

'Where are you now, then?' he says.

I smile ironically. 'Manvers Road bookies.'

* * *

I stand in the doorway and look inside. Manvers Road bookies, the place where it all began. I remember that day, over two years ago now, as though it was yesterday. Blown inside off the street, taking refuge from the storm. Meeting

One- Armed for the first time and asking him to help me place a bet, to help pass the time until my clothes dried out. A fiver to win on Raindancer. Gazing up at the big screen, the gates flying open and the two minutes that followed, after which nothing in my life would be quite the same again. The hairs standing up on the back of my neck as Raindancer came from last to first to win. The buzz I felt at winning eighty quid and walking home with a smile on my face for first time since mum died.

I take a few steps inside. Much has changed. A gang of four in their early twenties, all tracksuits and hoodies, hover around an FOBT machine. None of them bat an eye-lid upon my arrival. No one is watching the racing. I check the time on the wall. Two-fifty-eight. I look up at the big screen. The runners are circling behind the gate. I notice Ellie and Star biding their time out the back and my heart skips a beat.

I turn towards the counter and that's when I notice it. Des' stool, unoccupied in its usual place at the end of the betting counter, as though awaiting his arrival. Des' stool, a symbol alluding to dozens of magical afternoons spent down here. I walk over and place my hands on the backrest. As I do, an idea strikes me – to have a bronze plaque made up and fitted to the back of it, with the inscription, *'Des James sat here.'*

* * *

I turn and face the big screen again. As the stall handlers go about their work, I notice the shop manager, Glen's replacement for the day, approach me. He has greasy, shoulder length black hair and a ring through his nose.

'Are you going to have a bet?' he says, a little testily.

'I thought I might just watch this race and then be on my way – if it's all the same to you?'

He studies me a moment longer, risk assessing me, then shrugs his shoulders. 'I'll ring it off and get back to my book, then?' he says, with a faint smile.

I nod – and leaning on the back of Des' stool, look up as the last horse is loaded into the gate.

* * *

Tommo's voice booms over the shop tannoy. 'Racing to time at Colwick Park! Racing, Colwick Park!'

I hone in on stall five as the gates fly open. 'Hold on to your hats,' I whisper under my breath to Des. Ellie and Star shoot out of the stalls in a blur of green and red and make it across to the inside rail.

'And they're off in the Desmond James 1955 Champion Apprentice Jockey of Barbados Memorial Handicap over six furlongs,' blasts Tommo. 'Manvers Road Star breaks well and leads the field. It's Manvers Road Star in the green silks with red stars, from City Lights in the all pink with purple cap. Joint favourites Fingal's Cave and Pat's Choice are waited with out the back.' A bead of sweat appear on my forehead. Tommo forges on. 'They're approaching half way and Ellie McGovern has Manvers Road Star in a good rhythm, scraping paint against the rail. On they go at a good clip, approaching the four pole. Young apprentice Ellie McGovern is going to try to steal this from the front!'

'Go on Ellie,' I whisper under my breath.

Tommo is in full flight. 'They enter the final furlong and here comes Fingal's Cave with a promising run. Stalking her, Pat's Choice in the red and black quarters. Fingal's Cave and Pats Choice are closing down on Manvers Road Star on her inside with every stride!'

I tighten my grip on the back of Des' stool, my heart

racing. 'There's a couple of hundred yards to go and it's three horses in a line! Has Manvers Road Star got enough left in the tank?' booms Tommo. I watch through a gap in my webbed fingers. 'It's Fingal's Cave from Manvers Road Star, with Pats Choice finishing best of all! Pats Choice edges ahead of Fingal's Cave, Manvers Road Star is beaten back in third.' I turn away. *'Or is she?'* asks Tommo. I turn back.

That's when I witness something as intuitively beautiful as it is extraordinary. No Dayjur style antics from Star today. Having anticipated the late arrival of horses on her blind right side, Star responds to Ellie's urgings and musters one final winning challenge.

'YEESSSS!' I punch both fists into the air. *'She did it, Des!'* My heart is thumping in my chest like a hammer. I jump off the stool and run to the exit, in need of some air. 'YES, YES, YES!' I shout, stood in the doorway. I go to light a cigarette, my hands trembling, adrenaline pumping and then think again. No more smoking. I quit. I look both ways along Manvers Road. It's six minutes past three. The traffic has long since cleared. *I hope West Brom play Forest off the park,* I think to myself. My mobile phone starts ringing. I press answer. Duke's voice booms down the line.

'Bloody hell, Andy! She did it! Isn't it brilliant?'

My eyes well up. 'It is. It's … unreal!'

Duke continues. 'You've got to get up here!'

'I'm on my way!' I shout.

'Okay!' Duke rings off.

I head to Trent Car Taxis two doors along, floating on a cloud. I get into an awaiting cab and smile broadly at the driver. 'Colwick Park Racecourse, please.'

BIOGRAPHY

Jon Franklin was born in Harrow, Greater London, in 1963. *Manvers Road Star* is his second novel, the sequel to his debut *Shouting The Odds*, published in 2021. The inspiration for his writing comes from thirty years' experience of the racing and betting industry, ten years as an employee of William Hill, followed by twenty-two years as a professional racecourse photographer.

Jon got his first job at William Hill in 1987. It was his first experience of the racing and betting industry, a world that has fascinated him ever since. Jon's other passion in life is photography and following a rethink about his future, he successfully applied for a place on the photography degree course at Nottingham Trent University in 1994, where he supported himself financially while working for William Hill part-time.

During his penultimate year at university, *The Independent on Saturday* Magazine published a portfolio of his photographs that documented racecourse life in Britain, which helped to launch a successful freelance career. Over the twenty years that followed he provided a photographic service for sixteen of the UK and Ireland's racecourses, Aintree, Ascot, Cheltenham, Epsom, Newmarket and Goodwood among them. After relocating to Sweden in 2000, he acquired new clients such as Jägersro, Täby and Övrevoll while continuing to freelance in the UK and Ireland.

Jon's debut novel *Shouting The Odds* is the first work of British fiction with a high street betting shop as it's backdrop. It received positive reviews in the Racing Post and Sporting Life and the book was the subject of an interview by Simon Nott on behalf of Star Sports, as part of his excellent Betting People series. Before making a start on *Manvers Road Star*, with the encouragement of writer for Television and Film Stan Hey, Jon wrote a screenplay version of *Shouting The Odds*, in which he is trying to garner interest from television and film production companies.

Jon lives in Malmö with his wife Annika, where he works in the hospitality business.

AUTHORS NOTE

My parents shared a general indifference towards horse racing, so when I returned to north west London in 1987 following a backpacking trip around Europe and found a job in a betting shop, I think they were more relieved than concerned. Responding to a 'staff needed, apply within' sign in the window of my local William Hill, I was offered an interview the following day. It went well - I was offered a job and started work the following Monday. On the same day that I applied to Hills, I responded to a similar sign in the window of my local Sainsbury's. Fortunately, Hills got back to me first and in doing so, spared me a far less appealing future in the fruit and vegetable section of my local supermarket.

I enjoyed working at the bookies from day one, even if I was expected to work most Saturdays. My day off was usually on a Wednesday. On one such Wednesday, I woke up with an overwhelming urge to try my luck on the customer side of the betting shop counter. Later that morning, I walked into my local Arthur Prince and put on a one pound each-way treble. All three horses won and I pocketed one hundred and fifty-four pounds. Michael Tabor, owner of the Arthur Prince chain before he sold up and joined Coolmore, wouldn't have been amused. Talk about beginners luck! From that day onwards in a betting shop in north west London, my life would never be quite the same. It was, if you like, my very own 'Andy Cooper moment.'

In my author notes at the back of *Shouting The Odds*, I write about which events in the book are based on fact and which ones are fictional. I would like to do the same here with *Manvers Road Star*. There has never been a Manvers Road in Sneinton, though there is a Manvers *Street* and it is along this parade of shops that the betting shop I write about once stood. In the mid 1990s, I used to sometimes work there. Next door was a taxi rental firm. A stairwell ran between the two properties, at the top of which was a dodgy looking massage parlour and either side of that private flats. The betting shop manager was a *Goth* called Gordon, who had long, greasy black hair and a ring through his lip and was covered from head-to-toe in tattoos. The betting shop is long gone. Apparently, a micro-brewery stands in its place today. The Chinese takeaway restaurant two doors along is still there, though it was never called the Flying Dragon and its proprietors aren't superstitious horse bettors; not to my knowledge anyway. Like all of the characters in my books, Lee and Sammy Chan are fictional – though there is nothing made up about the King William pub, better known as the 'King Billy' to locals, from where I am glad to write pints are still served to this day.

The character Ray Baldwin is a mixture of two Nottinghamshire trainers, Roy Bowring and Jeremy Glover. The former is based at Edwinstowe and Jeremy Glover used to train from stables at Worksop, from where he sent out the winner of the Cambridgeshire Handicap four times between 1987 and 1996. Though I have never met Jeremy Glover, I did spend an afternoon in April 1994 with Roy Bowring, at his Fir Tree Farm stables. Probably out of curiosity more than anything, Roy agreed to me visiting his yard to take some photographs for a documentary project I was working on. At the time, he hadn't long been training a filly called Broadstairs Beauty, sent to him by her owner from Jonjo O'Neil's yard. Roy Bowring improved her greatly, training her to win seven races and place a further nine times from twenty-eight starts - including a run in the 1995 Stewards Cup at Goodwood. The day I visited, I watched Roy put Broadstairs Beauty through her paces ahead of a race at Colwick Park later that month. I got some good photographs, of which I later sent him duplicate prints. Some of them appeared in a photo feature of my work in *The Independent on Saturday* magazine, a few months later. One particular memory stick's in my mind from that afternoon. After I had taken my last photograph, Roy offered to drive me back to Edwinstowe Station. On the journey, the conversation turned to betting. With a barrage of expletives, he gave me his opinion of the betting shops in the area, none of whom any longer accepted his bets. Reserving his strongest language for his opinion of the manager of his local William Hill, I stayed tight-lipped about the identity of my part-time employer, for fear of being ejected from the passenger seat in the middle of the Sherwood Forest.

There is nothing fictitious about Belper, the one-eyed racehorse who inspires Ray Baldwin to nurture Star back into training. Belper ran on the flat in the 1970s. That said, I am not able to verify everything I found out about him as fact. What I do know is that he was trained for a Lady Manton by John Dunlop from his stables in the grounds of Arundel Castle. Neither am I sure whether Belper lost the sight in his right eye during his career or before it, but he definitely did at some stage – which explain his liking for left turning tracks such as Brighton and Epsom. Belper was usually partnered in his races by Ron Hutchinson. Remarkably, Belper won six races at Brighton, presumably with just his left eye intact. The fact that he even won a single race with just one eye made it plausible to me, to have a one-eyed Star run at Wolverhampton in my story.

As many readers will know, Garrison Savannah racecourse is a real racecourse. It is situated within the historic Garrison area of Barbados, just outside the capital Bridgetown and is known internationally for the annual Barbados Gold Cup, run over six furlongs. Unfortunately, Hurricane Janet was real too. The 1955 flat season at Garrison Savannah was abandoned after she struck Barbados in September of that year. Hurricane Janet remains one of the strongest hurricanes recorded in the history of the region and though Barbados suffered fewer fatalities than other countries in the Caribbean and beyond, it caused long term infrastructural damage to the island. Pebbles Beach is also a real place, situated just a short walk from the racecourse. Though I am not sure whether it still goes on today, some horse grooms who work at racing stables in the area used to bath the horses in their care at the beach after racing. A quick search on You Tube and you will be able to watch videos of this for yourself.

Horse racing has taken place at Colwick Park Racecourse since 1892. For anyone interested in reading a detailed account of its history, I can recommend the amusingly titled *A Touch of Colwick* by Grenville Davies (ISBN 1-874 4645 -03-05). Located three kilometres east of Nottingham city centre, the first time I visited was for a jumps meeting before they switched exclusively to flat racing. On a wet, blustery, winters afternoon, David 'The Duke' Nicholson could be found in the members bar enjoying a pre-race drink, when he tipped his runner in the opening hurdles race. Twenty minutes later, it was sent off a very well backed 5/1 second favourite, before winning by about six lengths. I didn't become privy to this golden nugget of information until a mud-splattered, smiling Adrian McGuire dismounted in the winners enclosure, when someone I knew from a Hills shop in town sidled over to me and told me about the tip. 'Did yer back it, n' all?' he asked. Trying hard to conceal my disappointment, I just looked at him blankly. While he'd been in the right place at the right time, I'd been stood under a faulty umbrella taking photographs in a rain-sodden parade ring. That'll teach me.

I returned to Colwick Park several years later as a photographer. I ran a business at the time providing photographs for racecourse websites and brochures. My visits to Colwick Park were always for the same well-attended meeting in July. The Jockey Club fixture list couldn't have been kinder. On the Saturday I worked at Colwick Park and the following day I would work at Market Rasen's big Summer Jumps fixture. I was offered accommodation at both courses. At Colwick Park, this meant staying at a hostel originally intended for travelling stable staff. It is situated on the opposite side of the racecourse to the grandstand, a stone throw from the one-mile start, just outside the outer rail. A racecourse groundsmen would let me into the place before I started working. With so many runners trained locally to the racecourse for that meeting, there was little demand for an overnight bed, meaning I was often the hostels only guest. Leaving my case in my room, I would walk back across the racecourse and start work. Conveniently, the 'lucky last' was always a one-mile handicap. That's where I would usually round off my evening's work, with some landscapes across the course of the horses and jockeys circling behind the stalls in near silhouette, as the summer light faded. Once the race was under away, I would head to the bar of the Colwick Hall Hotel, just a two-minute walk from the hostel for a well-earned pint. Happy Days. On the subject of places to go for a drink near to Colwick Park, in chapter seven of *Manvers Road Star*, Andy takes Rita to the Starting Gate pub. With a name like that, I admit that it sounds as though I made it up, but I can assure you that I didn't. The Starting Gate pub is at the very far end of the home straight, where the beer garden virtually backs on to the six-furlong start (hence the name).

There is nothing made up about Dunstall Park Racecourse in Wolverhampton of course and from the early stages of writing *Manvers Road Star*, I knew it was the perfect place in the book for the betting coup on 'Star'. There's just something about the place. At evening meetings, beams of light from the floodlights fuse with a hundred different florescent colours, providing an otherworldly, twilight ambience. On Saturday night meetings in the 90s, the glass fronted grandstand restaurant was always busy and the on-course Holiday Inn fully booked. At one such meeting, the scent of horses, grimy banknotes and booze in my nostrils, I wandered down to the inside rail. After the adrenaline rush of watching a fiercely competitive handicap, I gazed up the brightly lit home straight. Squinting my eyes, suddenly I felt I was back at Happy Valley Racecourse on Hong Kong Island, somewhere I was fortunate enough to visit the previous year. Perhaps I'd just had too much to drink and the black country accents soon brought me back to reality. Dunstall Park: I think you either love the place or you don't, which leads me nicely to the last fact or fiction question from the pages of *Manvers Road Star* – the one you have all been waiting for me to answer. Was there really ever a Tom Jones impersonator who sang live after racing? Of course there was – and whether or not he was to everyone's taste, just like Manvers Road Star's performances in her races, he never once failed to give his best. Thank you for reading *Manvers Road Star.* I hope you enjoyed reading it, as much as I enjoyed writing it.

ACKNOWLEDGEMENTS

My deepest love and gratitude to my wife, Annika, for your patience, love and unwavering support – not to mention your excellent beta reading skills.

* * *

Heartfelt thanks to fellow author, horse racing enthusiast and friend, Martin Ross. Your wisdom and editorial advice have helped make *Manvers Road Star* a better novel.

* * *

Special thanks to writer for Television and Film, Stan Hey, whose enthusiasm for *Shouting The Odds* inspired me to write this sequel.

* * *

Special thanks to trusted beta reader and friend Mike Box.

* * *

Sincere thanks to Sam Hardy for your review of *Shouting The Odds* in the Racing Post.

* * *

A special thank you to Dave Ord for your review of *Shouting The Odds* in the Sporting Life.

* * *

Heartfelt thanks to Liz Ampairee, for your assistance in helping to get the Racing Post Book Shop to stock *Shouting The Odds*.

* * *

Sincere thanks to betting journalist par excellence Simon Nott, for your review of *Shouting The Odds*, for promoting it to your followers and for interviewing me for the Star Sports #BettingPeople series.

* * *

A big thank you to Grade One winning owner and National Hunt breeder Carl Hinchy, for promoting *Shouting The Odds* to your followers on social media.

* * *

Special thanks to Stephen Harris, Racing Editor at BettingExpert, for the Q and A interview and for promoting *Shouting The Odds* on social media.

* * *

Heartfelt thanks to horse racing journalist Andrew Mount, for giving so freely of your time in helping authenticate details of Andy's betting coup in *Manvers Road Star*.

* * *

A collective thank you to all of the contributors to the Betfair community thread, 'Does anyone hear remember Belper?' Most of the background information I was able to find about John Dunlop's one-eyed Brighton specialist, I found here.

* * *

A special acknowledgement to Tom Byrne, Head of Racing and Betting at The British Horse Racing Authority, with regards to race declarations and the draw.

* * *

A big thank you to *Shouting The Odds* reader and Nottingham resident Dave Roper, for your help in making Chapter Fifty ring true.

* * *

Special thanks to Pip Kirkby, the former Managing Director of Jockey Club Racecourses East, for hiring my services as a racecourse photographer at Colwick Park and Market Rasen, long after I had left the UK. The photographs I took on your behalf not only led to other Jockey Club race-courses hiring me, your commissions also enabled my return to Nottingham, a town I will always hold close to my heart.

* * *

Special thanks to film maker and director Shane Meadows,

whose talk on scriptwriting in Nottingham in the mid-90s inspired me to write *Shouting The Odds*.

* * *

Heartfelt love to my late grandfather Geoffrey Corder, for passing on your love for writing.

CAST OF CHARACTERS

Andy Cooper - Sneinton born and bred 25-year-old postman and the story's protagonist. Pies (Notts County) fan and regular at Manvers Road bookies.

Rita Ferguson – 24-year-old former cashier at Manvers Road bookies. Qualified social worker and Andy's girlfriend.

Des James – Barbados born retired Nottingham bus driver. Manvers Road bookies veteran. Widowed five years previously by Shirelle. Father to Marsha and grandpa to Kyle.

Marsha James – Des' daughter. Nottingham born and raised divorcee. Lives in Birmingham.

Kyle James – Marsha's teenage son. Lives alternate weeks with his dad, Del.

Duke – Middle aged divorcee. Sneinton based solicitor and keen punter. Another stalwart of Manvers Road bookies.

Laura – Duke's girlfriend. Marketing Manager at Colwick Park Racecourse. Niece of Ray Baldwin.

Ray Baldwin – Racehorse trainer at Nine Elms Stables, Edwinstowe, North Nottinghamshire.

Ellie McGovern – 22- year-old Dublin born stable assistant at Nine Elms Stables.

Big Les – Geordie former miner. Another Manvers Road Bookies regular.

Glen – Long serving manager of Manvers Road Bookies. Keen punter.

One-Armed – Security guard and racing fan. A regular at Manvers Road bookies. In his early thirties, married to Collette, with two young children. Real name Bruce.

Lee Chan – Chinese born proprietor of The Flying Dragon Takeaway Restaurant, two doors along from Manvers Road Bookies. Dedicated yet superstitious punter - racing selections informed by lucky Chinese colours and numbers.

Sammy Chan – Lee Chan's son, Sneinton born and bred manager of The Flying Dragon. Keen punter like his dad.

Printed in Great Britain
by Amazon

60883186R00170